Mistaken for Sunbathers

By the Same Author

Novels
The Restraint of Beasts
All Quiet on the Orient Express
Three to See the King
The Scheme for Full Employment
Explorers of the New Century
The Maintenance of Headway
A Cruel Bird Came to the Nest and Looked In
The Field of the Cloth of Gold
The Forensic Records Society
Tales of Muffled Oars
The Trouble with Sunbathers
Sunbathers in a Bottle

Stories
Once in a Blue Moon
Only When the Sun Shines Brightly
Screwtop Thompson and Other Tales

Mistaken for Sunbathers

Magnus Mills

QUOQS

Quoqs Publishing for Magnus Mills

First Published 2022

Kindle Direct Publishing

Cover designed by Richard Moody

Cover illustration by Rawpixel

For Sue

1

We'd only travelled a few miles when I started wondering how I could rid myself of the three sunbathers. This might sound churlish but actually I felt I owed them no debt of gratitude. They'd only stopped to pick me up because I was wearing a beach robe! They plainly didn't recognise me and I guessed my appearance must have altered during my period of internment. True enough I'd developed a slight tan and my hair was tousled but it didn't mean I was one of them (which was presumably what they thought). Nevertheless I'd accepted the offer of a ride and I was now heading west in a black four-door sedan. Lenny and Zoony were sprawled in the back seat and Terry was behind the wheel. They were seemingly unchanged since I'd last seen them. Their announcement that they were 'going to the beach' told me they'd learned nothing from the turbulence of recent months. Great Britain was rapidly degenerating into a wilderness yet all they cared about was sunbathing.

Furthermore it was quite obvious that the black sedan didn't belong to them. No sooner had I climbed into the passenger seat than I noticed a large feather stuck in the dashboard. Whether they realised its significance was unclear but to my eyes it was a glaring piece of evidence. The rightful owner was Ambrose, a man who spent most of his waking hours providing assistance to other people. Admittedly he could be generous to a fault at times but even so I hardly imagined him simply handing his car over to those three. I concluded, therefore, that they must have obtained it through trickery. Most likely they'd left him stranded somewhere and for this reason I felt it was my duty to turn the tables on them.

It would be folly, however, to try and act immediately. Instead I needed to devise a scheme that would give me full control of the situation. From past experience I knew that Lenny, Zoony and Terry were unprincipled customers who could not be trusted from one minute to the next. They cared about nobody but themselves and if they once suspected my motives they'd doubtless abandon me at the wayside. Fortunately they were also rather slow on the uptake. They never considered the consequences of their deeds and if anything went wrong they always placed the blame on somebody else. Nor did they ever contemplate the future beyond the next twenty-four hours. With these facts in mind I was confident I could run circles around them. All it required was a little circumspection. Meanwhile I sat back and tried to enjoy the journey.

Terry's driving was predictably poor. He probably thought he was king of the road in the driving seat of a black four-door sedan, cruising along a deserted highway with all the windows open, but actually he wasn't. He was barely in control of the vehicle and drove mostly with just one finger on the wheel. He didn't bother keeping left but instead hogged the middle lane whilst totally ignoring the mirrors and the speedometer. Apparently his mind was elsewhere.

'What we ought to do,' he said at length, 'is go and live in a lighthouse.'

His words weren't addressed to me, of course. He was speaking to Lenny and Zoony who both remained motionless in the back seat with their eyes closed and the breeze wafting over them. After a few languid seconds Lenny stirred.

'Brilliant idea,' he murmured. 'Right next to the beach.'

'We could all have our own rooms,' added Zoony. 'Up a spiral staircase.'

'Parties every night,' said Terry.

I'd heard them indulge in similar small talk on previous occasions and they never failed to astonish me. Their detachment from reality was pitiful. Surely they must have known that the chances of finding an empty lighthouse were practically nil. Back in the days of the purchase a mass exodus had taken place when virtually the entire population of the British Isles migrated to the coast. Every piece of property imaginable had been snapped up by developers and converted into homes for the newcomers. Seaside pavilions, fishermen's cottages, customs sheds, warehouses and lifeboat stations had all come under the hammer but none were as widely sought after as the disused lighthouses. The lucky few who got hold of them regarded them as prize possessions and they certainly weren't going to relinquish them to a bunch of itinerant sunbathers in a black sedan. Yet here were Lenny, Zoony and Terry making plans for living in a lighthouse as though it was a matter of course!

I listened with incredulity as they developed the idea. From what I could gather they knew some women at the coast who could be prevailed upon to move into the lighthouse and provide recreation when required. Facilities would include a sun deck, an icebox for the beer and a portable barbecue. They clearly envisioned a sunbathers' paradise. The lighthouse would be painted white (not by them, needless to say, but by somebody else). Their days would be spent idling on the nearby beach and their nights given over to merrymaking.

In some respects I was tempted to go along with it all. Fantasy or not, the prospect of such an existence certainly had its attractions. Moreover, I could easily be swayed by the sun's stubborn refusal to stop shining. By my reckoning it was now very late in the summer but still the season showed no indication of coming to an end. One cloudless day was followed unfailingly by the next so maybe the sunbathers were correct in following their instincts.

A warm climate would also explain how a girl on an elephant could roam freely through the midland counties accompanied by some zebras, some ostriches and a young giraffe. She'd been travelling in this manner for at least a year and nobody had noticed except me. In hindsight I realised I should have left her to her own devices instead of broadcasting her presence to everyone I met. Now she was the subject of a national hue and cry and I was largely to blame. My attempts to make contact with her had failed repeatedly. I'd only been trying to alert her to the peril she faced but she'd proved to be unapproachable. All I could do now was attempt to draw attention away from her in the hope she'd be left alone to enjoy some peace and quiet.

Oddly enough, one of the few people who'd seen any sign of the roving menagerie was currently lounging in the back seat of the black sedan. Many weeks ago I'd overheard Terry and Zoony teasing Lenny because he thought he'd spotted an ostrich out in the fields. Personally I was inclined to believe him but I'd kept my opinion to myself. Now that I found myself in their company once more I decided it would be best to make no mention of the girl on the elephant. They were bound to have known the story of Lee Montana and her supposed disappearance in Africa. If they discovered she was here in the British Isles they'd no doubt be keen to make her acquaintance. This was plainly out of the question. The last thing she needed was to be chased around the countryside by the three sunbathers.

For the time being, however, they were content to delude themselves about living in a lighthouse. Their vision was jumbled and incoherent to say the least. One minute the fictitious lighthouse was perched at the top of a cliff; next it was situated in a secluded cove; then finally on a rocky outcrop surrounded by lapping seawater (this last option was summarily dismissed because it would be inconvenient if they ever wanted to go to a snack bar). Meanwhile they observed with some urgency that they all needed new flip flops and sunglasses. Without these items, apparently, life was a 'nightmare'. In due course their enthusiasm waned and the discussion faded away.

All I heard now was the purring of the engine as we bowled along that highway. I looked out for signposts which might tell us how far it was to the coast but there were none (they'd all succumbed to rust). There was only the empty tarmac vanishing into the distance.

Except that it was not quite empty.

Up ahead of us I noticed a kind of break in the shimmering haze. The sun was glinting on some object in the westbound carriageway. As we drew nearer I saw that it was actually a very slow-moving vehicle resembling a glasshouse on wheels. It was minding its own business, creeping painstakingly along the left-hand lane at no more than 20mph and was hardly obstructing anybody. Nonetheless, the sunbathers decided to have some fun with it. The instant he saw the vehicle Terry emitted an ear-splitting whoop and put his foot down. This alerted Lenny and Zoony who sat up in their seats to see what was going on before both scrambling towards the nearside window and sticking their heads out. By now we were gaining rapidly on the other vehicle. The driver must have spotted us in his mirror because he now offered even more space by moving a little further to the left. He needn't have bothered. Terry clearly intended to 'buzz' his hapless victim and he now put on an additional spurt of speed while pressing hard on the horn. We passed with inches to spare and at the same moment Lenny and Zoony cried 'Yaaaah!' as loudly as they could. The other vehicle seemed to shy away from us as if flinching to avoid a blow from a bully. Naturally I wished to play no part in this jape so I sat sullenly staring through the windscreen. A few seconds later it was all over and the glasshouse on wheels was receding behind us.

Lenny and Zoony peered gleefully through the rear window.

'It'll take him days to get there at that speed,' Lenny announced, 'and all for nothing.'

I wasn't sure what he meant by his remark. Obviously he can't have known who was driving the other vehicle or where was he going (if indeed it was a he). We'd sped by at such a velocity that we'd barely caught a glimpse of anybody inside. Therefore I assumed Lenny was simply making a generalisation.

It struck me that he and his pals didn't really know where they were going themselves. They'd made vague references to 'the beach' and 'the coast' (not to mention lighthouses) but patently they had no precise destination. I suspected they were merely following the sun, which was all good and well while the road went in the same direction. After another few miles, though, we came to a point where it divided. As usual there were no signposts to tell us whether to take the left or right fork. Terry slewed the car onto the hard shoulder and stopped.

'Which way?' he asked.

'Dunno,' said Lenny. 'I thought you knew.'

'No.'

'Nor me,' said Zoony.

'Technically we're still in the midland counties,' I ventured, 'so if we make a mistake now we could end up going miles out of our way.'

Terry glared at me.

'You trying to be funny?' he demanded.

'No.'

'So what's all this about the midland counties?'

'That's where we are.'

'Aren't we almost at the coast then?'

'No.'

'Well how far is it?'

'At least a hundred miles,' I said. 'Possibly more.'

'You're joking.'

Terry was plainly devastated at the prospect of not going to the beach any time soon. The look of despondency that crossed his face when I broke the news almost made me feel sorry for him. Then again I distinctly remembered a similar conversation on our very first encounter. At that time I'd gone to great lengths to explain to the sunbathers that the midland counties were some distance from the coast. It wasn't my fault if they'd forgotten already. Once again I was astounded by their cluelessness but I realised I had to be careful what I said. They weren't the sort who could readily brook criticism. If I got on the wrong side of them they would have no qualms about leaving me behind.

'Maybe there's a map in the glove compartment,' I suggested.

Knowing how meticulous Ambrose was in the upkeep of his car I presumed there would be a map or road atlas stored somewhere. On inspection, however, the glove compartment contained only a service manual for the black sedan.

'I can go and look in the boot if you like.'

'Alright,' said Terry.

As he spoke I thought I saw him glance in the rear view mirror. It looked as if he was trying to catch the eye of one or other of his friends in the back seat. I opened the door and got out and immediately the car accelerated away in a cloud of dust. It screeched to a halt about thirty yards further along the hard shoulder. I then heard raucous laughter coming from within. I strolled towards the car and again it shot away and stopped after thirty yards. More laughter. This time I remained where I was and half a minute later it reversed back to where I was standing. When I was certain they'd finished fooling around I opened the boot. Inside were a tow rope, a toolbox, a first aid kit and a large hamper full of lunchboxes. There was no map. I slammed the boot shut and walked around the side of the car.

'Nothing of interest,' I said.

(I made no mention of the lunchboxes.)

'Well I'm not taking the blame if we go the wrong way,' said Terry, 'and I've had enough of driving. It's too much like hard work.'

He got out and wandered over to the grass verge. Zoony and Lenny went and joined him and they all stood side-by-side facing away from me. I could hear them murmuring to one another. When they came back Terry nodded to me and indicated the driving seat.

'Alright,' he said. 'You can sing for your supper.'

The three of them climbed into the back seat while I got behind the wheel and adjusted the mirrors to my personal requirements.

'You don't have to do all that!' snapped Zoony. 'Just drive.'

I ignored him and eased the car off the hard shoulder and onto the tarmac. Someone behind me yawned. I gathered speed and approached the fork in the road.

'Which way?' I asked.

'Who cares?' said Lenny.

I interpreted this as an abdication of responsibility and chose the left fork. There were a few more murmurs but no further comments were made directly to me. When we reached fifty miles per hour I depressed a lever beneath the steering wheel and the car settled smoothly into cruising mode. It was capable of much higher speeds but fifty would do for now. Still there came no word from my passengers. A glimpse in the rear view mirror told me the three sunbathers were lying back with their eyes closed. Seemingly they were all tired out. I lowered the sun visor and headed into the west.

2

Darkness had fallen when I rolled to a halt in front of a disused service station. I switched off the headlights, cut the engine and removed the keys from the ignition. Quietly I got out and went round to the back of the car, opened the boot and took out a lunchbox. Nobody stirred when I got back into the car. They were all sound asleep. I put the lunchbox under my seat and resumed the journey.

I had no idea where we were or what kind of country we were travelling through. For several hours I'd been following a route that I assumed would eventually bring us to the coast but of course I couldn't be sure. All I knew was that there were fewer buildings around us and that they were increasingly more scattered. The service station where I'd stopped had plainly been out of use for a good while. According to the fuel gauge there was a quarter of a tank of petrol remaining. Obviously I had no inkling where Ambrose had last filled up but I guessed there was a better chance of finding a fuel outlet by the coast. For this reason it was now imperative we got there rather than simply a whim of the three sunbathers.

They'd been fast asleep for hours but I predicted they'd be hungry when they woke up: hence my preparedness with the lunchbox. I'd seen in the past how easily they lapsed into dependence on other people so I'd decided to take advantage of the fact. They were already treating me like a servant, instructing me to sing for my supper and so forth, yet I was sure it wouldn't be long until I had them eating out of my hand.

I switched on the radio and scanned hopefully through the dial. As usual there was nothing along the wavebands except a fuzzy silence. Such had been the case for a few years now. All the inland radio services closed down when the purchase came into effect and the population migrated to the seaside. I was aware, however, that a few offshore stations continued to cater for people living on the coast. If I could pick up any of these I'd know I'd chosen the correct course. For the time being I heard nothing but I made a mental note to try again later.

Why I found it necessary to keep driving through the night was difficult to explain. As far as I knew the sunbathers of Great Britain were no longer being rounded up by the park authority so there was little urgency in that respect. If Lenny, Zoony and Terry were mentioned on any other 'wanted' list I was yet to hear of it. Moreover, I didn't count myself as a fugitive. I wasn't on the run from anybody. On the other hand there would be no harm in putting some distance between ourselves and the midland counties.

Despite the pleasant surroundings my sojourn there had been a source of great disappointment. The so-called 'independent settlement' on which I'd staked so much had turned out to be a complete sham while its supposed oppressors had proved hopelessly ineffective. Anyone caught between the two sides was liable to be compromised in one way or another. For this reason it was best to just keep moving.

Not that that my three travelling companions would appreciate my efforts. As always they remained oblivious to the trouble other people went to on their behalf. Ever since I'd known them their every need had been provided for (sometimes by complete strangers) and it was a state of affairs they'd swiftly become accustomed to. Therefore they could hardly be held to blame when they took everything for granted. I was the latest in a long line of nursemaids and it might even be argued that I had a duty of care towards them. My task was to

21

keep them fed and watered and convey them safely to the coast. The rewards, I presumed, would come later. In the meantime I should exercise patience.

A movement in the back seat informed me that at least one person was beginning to wake up.

'Who opened this window?' said Terry. 'It's freezing.'

(Actually it was nowhere near freezing: it was a balmy evening in late summer.)

'You're sitting next to it,' murmured Zoony. 'You must of left it open.'

'Well someone should've closed it. I've got a stiff neck now.'

Terry continued moaning until Lenny told him to shut up. There was no more playful banter between them and I guessed immediately why they were all so grouchy.

'Who's ready for some supper?' I enquired.

'Yeah, alright,' said Lenny. 'What you got?'

'Hang on a sec.'

I pulled over to the side of the road and stopped. Reaching beneath my seat I produced the lunchbox and opened the lid before selecting one item each for the three of them.

'Where'd you get this?' asked Zoony.

'I collected it earlier in the evening.'

'Any ketchup?'

'I'm afraid not.'

'They should of supplied ketchup.'

'Who?'

'The people at the snack bar.'

I was about to correct Zoony when I realised it would quite useful if he and his buddies thought I'd obtained the lunchbox at a snack bar (they clearly had no knowledge of the hoard of boxes in the boot). I offered them second helpings and took something for myself. There was also a bottle of water which unfortunately we all had to share. It was finished off by Terry.

'Next time get something with some fizz in it,' he snapped, throwing the empty bottle out of the window.

'Better pick that up,' I said. 'We shouldn't leave it lying in the road.'

'I'm not picking it up,' he replied.

'Alright.'

I got out and picked up the bottle before stalking off into the night. With the car keys safely in my pocket I continued walking for about a mile. It was good to stretch my legs and generally loosen up after the long drive. The moon was out and eventually I found a grassy embankment at the side of the road. The evening was still warm so I laid down for a peaceful doze. Two hours later I returned to the car and found the three sunbathers in an agitated state.

'Where've you been?' demanded Terry.

'Looking for a litter bin,' I replied.

'Did you find one?'

'No.'

I handed him the empty bottle.

'Let's go,' I said, sliding behind the wheel.

Without another word they settled down behind me and we continued on our way. I was feeling rather pleased with myself. My brief repose had left me thoroughly refreshed and I was looking forward to a relaxing drive right through the night and on until dawn. Even now the first streaks of daylight were appearing in the sky ahead. As the stars vanished one by one I suddenly felt a profound sense of expectation. I was certain my plans would come to fruition within the next few hours. All I had to do was find somewhere appropriate to deposit the three sunbathers and then I could see about returning the car to Ambrose. The drawback, of course, was that I didn't know where he was. After some consideration I then developed a secondary course of action whereby I would make myself temporary custodian of the vehicle until such a time as I could resume contact with him. The continuing silence from the back seat suggested that Lenny, Zoony and Terry had all drifted back to sleep. I drove steadily onward and the horizon started slowly turning pink. For some reason, however, my former optimism was gradually displaced by an uneasiness that I couldn't quite put my finger on. The car was running perfectly and really there should have been nothing to concern me. Even so I was beset by an odd feeling of disquietude as the sky ahead of me brightened and the sun began to rise.

All at once I realised I was going east instead of west! The road I'd chosen must have curved imperceptibly to the left as the miles went by and I'd failed to notice! I peered with alarm into the rear view mirror to make sure the three sunbathers were still at their slumbers. Luckily they were. Next I slowed down in readiness for a stealthy U-turn. It then struck me that going back the way we'd come would achieve nothing at all. Far better to proceed further along the same road until we reached a major junction where sensible choices could be made. I put the car back into cruising mode and resumed the journey as though nothing had happened.

The sole consolation for my mistake was that I was able categorically to confirm that we were now nearing the coast. It wasn't the kind of coast I was expecting but it was still the coast. As dawn broke I saw seabirds whirling over a distant shipping terminal. The land all around was low-lying and marshy and opened out into an immense bay. The sea air was pungent rather than bracing but nevertheless I enjoyed a brief surge of triumph. We were indeed approaching the coast! To our left there appeared a wide stretch of mud which I assumed to be an estuary at low tide. There was a narrow creek running through it where a number of boats lay at precarious angles. Various species of wildfowl pecked around in the shallows. Further out were sandbanks that glistened in the early morning sun.

The road was now running along a causeway with marker posts at regular intervals indicating the level of the sea. After another mile I saw a lay-by so I quietly pulled over. I got out of the car, carefully removed another lunchbox from the boot and hid it beneath the driving seat before pausing to take in the scenery. With the tide so far out it was difficult to determine where the estuary ended and the sea began. Likewise, the exact extent of the marshes was impossible to tell. The sandbanks were already beginning to dry in the sunshine and judging by the clear blue sky it was going to be another hot day.

The car's suspension creaked and next moment the radio began blaring loudly. A disembodied voice said 'Dogger, Fisher, Germ......' before becoming distorted and then disappearing altogether. A few seconds passed and then the voice said 'Viking, Forties……'

Someone inside the car gave a cry of frustration and the radio fell silent. A door swung open to reveal Terry leaning over from the back seat and jabbing various buttons on the dashboard.

'Why's there no music?' he wanted to know.

'Probably no demand,' I suggested.

'What?'

'Not enough listeners.'

'What about all the people on the beach?'

'We're not there yet.'

'What?'

Terry looked past me towards the bay and instantly his eyes widened.

'Mud!' he exclaimed. 'Mud's really good for your skin!'

I was inclined to point out that only certain types of mud were good for the skin but he was already clambering out of the car followed swiftly by his two comrades. They each carried a rolled-up towel which they laid on top of the sea wall. They then removed their beach robes and put them beside the towels before starting down towards the mud.

'Don't you want some breakfast first?' I asked.

'You can sort that out later,' said Zoony.

I watched as they padded across a margin of wet sand before plunging headlong into the mud. They horsed around until they were all encased from head to foot and then began splashing through the shallow water towards the nearest sandbank. It was probably further away than they thought because it took them a while to get there and they sunk deeper and deeper into the mud with every step. Still they persevered and I guessed they intended to dry out on the sandbank. Their voices seemed a long way off as they called excitedly to one another.

Here was the opportunity to end my association with Lenny, Zoony and Terry. My intention was to wait for half an hour or so until they'd warmed themselves and the caked mud had fallen from their bodies. When I was sure they were happily ensconced on their sandbank I would simply drive away. In the meantime I sat on the sea wall and enjoyed my share of the sunshine.

After about twenty minutes Zoony stood up and began waving his arms at me. Once he was sure he'd got my attention he pretended to eat with a spoon from an imaginary bowl. I gathered from these signals that he was instructing me to organise their breakfast. He clearly assumed I knew of a convenient snack bar located somewhere nearby. I decided to play him along. I nodded and pointed towards the road. He nodded in return and then lay down again. As a parting gesture I placed the lunchbox on the sea wall before getting into the car and starting up. I hooted the horn as I moved off but the three sunbathers failed to acknowledge me.

'You're on your own now,' I murmured. 'There's nobody going to help you.'

I eased onto the road and took it nice and slow. There was no particular hurry because I was yet to decide on my destination. That decision could wait until later. I was alone in a four-door black sedan and for the time being I wanted to make the most of my new-found freedom.

The causeway continued for another mile before ending abruptly at a T-Junction. A faded sign said ALL TRAFFIC with an arrow pointing right. Out of curiosity I turned left and after about fifty yards came to a dead end. The tarmac stopped at a low concrete wall with a safety railing running along the top. Nearby was a shelter that overlooked the mouth the estuary and I imagined the spot was once popular with sightseers and fishermen. I parked the car and strolled to the shelter for a better view. There was a coin-operated telescope but I couldn't even remember when I last possessed a coin. Instead I shaded my eyes and peered out. Straightaway I noticed that some of the outermost boats had come unstuck from the mud and were now riding gently on their moorings. Countless rivulets coursed between the remaining vessels and there seemed to be fewer sandbanks than before. I also noticed that the wildfowl had ceased wading in the shallows. I watched them flying inland and wondered what impelled them to go. The sun was shining brightly but a slight breeze had started to get up. All across the estuary there was water on the move. Sparkling waves were rushing in from the bay and the entrance to the creek was no longer visible. I remained gazing at the scene for several moments and then suddenly I realised what I was witnessing.

Very soon I was back in the car and speeding towards the causeway. Fortunately there was no other traffic on the road so I was able to put my foot down and got back to the lay-by in only a few minutes. The three sunbathers were still lying supine on their sandbank. They were apparently unaware of the approaching waters. I hooted the horn but there was no response so I parked the car and ran over to the sea wall.

'Hey!' I shouted.

No response.

'Hey!'

This time Zoony sat up. When he spotted me he began beckoning me to join them.

'Watch out!' I cried. 'The tide's coming in!'

He beckoned me again. Plainly my words hadn't carried far enough. It was also obvious that he expected me to deliver breakfast for the three of them.

I scrambled over the sea wall and started paddling towards the sandbank. By now it was actually the only sandbank above water but still they hadn't noticed. When I was halfway I stopped and pointed down the estuary. They glanced around them and at last they understood. Once I was certain they'd got the message I returned to the sea wall and sat down.

From my vantage point I could see that I'd only just got back in time. The rising waters swiftly engulfed the sandbank and were now swirling along the upper reaches of the creek. One by one the stranded boats floated free and then turned on their mooring ropes to face the current. Meanwhile Lenny, Zoony and Terry were wading ashore. They staggered up to the sea wall and asked where the nearest beach shower was. When I told them it was unlikely there were any showers close by they blamed me for being the bearer of bad news. They dried themselves as best they could and afterwards their towels were all sticky (which was also seemingly my fault).

They complained even more when I presented them with the lunchbox.

'This is the same as the last one,' said Lenny. 'You should've got a different sort.'

'With a fizzy drink,' said Terry.

'And I bet you didn't get any ketchup,' added Zoony.

'No,' I said. 'You'll have to do without.'

He glowered at me but said nothing more on the subject. I remembered I'd left the keys in the ignition so as a precaution I casually wandered back to the car and retrieved them. By now the incoming waters were lapping at the foot of the sea wall. The three sunbathers gazed across the estuary with unconcealed displeasure while they consumed the contents of the lunchbox. They didn't offer me a share so I went over and helped myself. Again nothing was said. Their peevishness was manifest but somehow I knew it wouldn't last forever. The sun was still shining and eventually its soothing rays took effect. They began laughing and joking about being stuck on the sandbank and then enquired how far it was to the next beach.

'There's a huge bay down the road,' I said, 'but the tide's in just now.'

'Doesn't matter,' said Terry. 'There's bound to be somewhere to sunbathe.'

With the decision thus made we returned to the black sedan. Needless to say I made sure I got there first and slid into the driving seat. A minute later we were cruising down the causeway.

3

It wasn't the kind of bay where people normally sunbathed. We turned onto the road that said ALL TRAFFIC and followed the seashore for about a mile. Instead of a sandy beach, however, all we saw were hundreds of huge boulders piled on top of one another. From what I could make out a vast quantity of sand had been washed into the estuary and clogged it up. I guessed these boulders were put there by civil engineers in the hope of halting the process. I tried explaining the theory to Lenny, Zoony and Terry but they weren't interested. They stared at the place where the beach should have been and bemoaned the fact that showers weren't provided. In case of any doubt a sign said DANGER: NO SWIMMING. For my part I thought the deserted bay had a certain appeal of its own.

Evidently there had been several attempts in the past to control the churning waves. As well as the boulders there was a breakwater further along the shore that projected into the sea. Also a massive concrete block at the water's edge whose purpose was unclear. I should have liked to do some exploring but in the present company this was more or less impossible. Therefore I simply pressed on.

What I needed to find was a beach resort with lots of amusements where I could safely abandon the sunbathers. There was nothing of the kind on this stretch of the coast. On the landward side the road ran through marshes with only a few scattered houses. I doubted very much if the local inhabitants would have wanted these three moving in next door to them.

For the moment they'd all fallen silent and I guessed their recent exertions had drained them of energy. Hopefully they'd soon drift off to sleep. I drove as smoothly as I could around the edge of the bay and after a few more miles we'd left the marshes behind. Now there was a high steel security fence on our left and I realised we'd reached the shipping terminal I'd seen from a distance. Suddenly we were passing overhead gantries, cranes, containers and administrative buildings. Lorries were turning in through the dock gates and at one point we had to wait at a railway level crossing as a goods train crossed over. It was odd to see all this economic activity after spending so much time in the interior: I'd forgotten that everything needed to be imported now that Great Britain had stopped making things. All the traffic was coming from the opposite direction and the road had widened considerably. Soon there were houses on either side and I could see people sunbathing in the gardens. I'd lost sight of the sea some time ago but I reckoned it had to be somewhere close by. Gradually the houses gave way to vast encampments of static caravans. I assumed these sites had been created to accommodate the population overflow following the mass migration to the coast. They went on for mile after mile and next to every caravan there was at least one person sunbathing. I pondered why they didn't simply go to the beach. Perhaps they were still wary of being rounded up by the park authority.

After a while, though, a secondary explanation came to mind. It was quite possible that my sense of direction had failed me once again and led me to stray away from the coast. The further we went the more likely this seemed. There were no shops at the roadside selling buckets and spades and similar beach accessories, no ice cream vans and certainly no gulls soaring overhead. The only positive indication lay in the names of the caravan sites. Each had an arch above its entrance emblazoned with a grand title: OCEAN SPRAY, SUMMER BREEZE, SANDY BAY, BAREFOOT ON THE BEACH and so forth. Finally we came to a site called SEA VIEW and this was sufficient to trigger a reaction in the back seat. Apparently my passengers were waking up.

'Sea View!' cried Terry. 'Let's go in there!'

I stopped opposite the entrance.

'You sure?' I asked.

'Yeah!' he replied. 'Come on! Hurry up!'

I turned in and proceeded along a narrow concrete road that ran between the rows of caravans. Everywhere we looked there were people lying on sun loungers. There was a neatly mown lawn around each caravan and I noticed they were all identical. Likewise their owners were barely distinguishable from one another. The women all wore bikinis and the men all sported colourful shorts. Almost every one of them had a bottle of suntan oil within easy reach. They stared at us as we went by and seemed rather displeased at our presence. It goes without saying that Lenny, Zoony and Terry were oblivious to their cool reception.

'This is just the sort of place,' enthused Lenny. 'Right by the beach.'

I wasn't so certain. The narrow road appeared to continue indefinitely with side turnings at regular intervals leading to yet more caravans. I was just about to suggest that we ask somebody the way when a horn beeped us from behind. I glanced in the mirror and saw a van flashing its headlights. It beeped its horn again so I slowed down and stopped. The van was similar to the type used by the park authorities when they were rounding up sunbathers. Lenny, Zoony and Terry took one look at it, grabbed their towels and jumped out of the car. A man in a straw hat emerged from the van and tried to speak to them but it was already too late. They ran away between the caravans and were swiftly lost from view.

The man approached me.

'Where do they think they're going?' he demanded.

'To the beach.'

'They'll be lucky,' he said. 'It's five and a half miles by road.'

'But the sign at the entrance said 'Sea View'.'

'That's just the name of the site.'

'Oh.'

'And anyway they're heading in the wrong direction.'

The man had a rather imperious manner and I concluded he must be a figure of local prominence.

'Are you from the park authority?' I enquired.

'No,' he said. 'I collect the rent for the caravans. Do you realise you're on private property?'

'Sorry, I was just dropping those three off.'

'So you're leaving now are you?'

'Yes.'

'Alright, well if you take the first left and then left again it'll take you around to the exit.'

'OK, thanks.'

He peered into the black sedan and his eyes settled on the large feather stuck in the dashboard.

'Where did you get that?' he asked

'It came with the car.'

'Well, I should get rid of it if I were you.'

'Why?'

'It could cause you a lot of trouble.'

'It's been alright so far.'

'Suit yourself.'

He bade me good day and I followed his directions. I lost count of the number of caravans I passed on the way out but it must have been in the hundreds. Noon was approaching and all the sun loungers were fully occupied. Eventually I reached the exit and turned back onto the main road. I passed a few more caravan sites after SEA VIEW but then they began to peter out. It appeared I was heading inland once more but I wasn't really bothered: I'd already decided that the coastal region was far too crowded for my liking. Soon I was passing factories, pubs, schools and residential areas all abandoned and overgrown with foliage. There was barely any oncoming traffic. I was now on a stretch of road where the tarmac was cracked, the white lines had faded and the signs were rusty. Nonetheless the road had an important feel to it as though it had once been a major thoroughfare. I continued another few miles and saw ahead of me an elaborate wrought iron gate. Next to it was a gatehouse. The gate bore a strong resemblance to the western gate where I'd worked as a gatekeeper all those months ago. I guessed this must be the eastern gate. I also knew that it wasn't a proper gate in the usual sense of the word. Actually it was one of four ceremonial gates inaugurated on the day that Great Britain was officially declared a national park. These gates were largely symbolic and were meant to be open to anyone who wished to pass through. The gate ahead of me was closed so I pulled up and waited for the gatekeeper to come and attend to it. A moment later the gatehouse door opened and a man emerged wearing a park authority uniform. He strolled over to the black sedan.

'Morning, sir,' he said. 'Is this your vehicle?'

'No,' I replied. 'I'm looking after it for someone.'

'The reason I ask is that we've had reports of a black sedan with a large feather stuck in the dashboard.'

'Ah yes,' I said. 'It's just here.'

I indicated the feather.

'Well, would you mind stepping into the gatehouse to answer one or two questions?'

'Suppose not.'

He showed me a lay-by where I could leave the car and then led the way inside and sat me down at a table.

'The name's Hartley,' he announced.

'Pleased to meet you.'

'Like a cup of tea?'

'That would be nice.'

'Sugar?'

'No thanks.'

Once he'd put the kettle on he sat down opposite me and opened a large book. He turned it towards me and leafed through the pages.

'Have you seen any of these on your travels?'

There were pictures of elephants, zebras, ostriches and giraffes.

'Yes,' I said. 'I saw them years ago at the zoo.'

'What about more recently?'

'It's hard to say.'

This interview promised to be difficult. I was reluctant to admit I'd seen any of the pictured animals because I wanted to protect Lee Montana and her roving menagerie. If I revealed too much it might lead to them being captured. It struck me that Hartley was carrying out his duties much more diligently than I ever did when I was in partnership with Rupert. We occasionally used to ask people if they'd noticed anything unusual in the course of their travels but we never went so far as to invite them into our gatehouse. Plainly a lot had changed since then. Moreover the park authority seemed to have advanced a long way in pursuit of its new goal. I realised too late that I should have heeded the advice of the man at the caravan site. I also regretted the route I'd chosen. The national park had numerous unsupervised entrances and exits (such as the one that had led me into the marshes) yet by some chance I'd managed to arrive at the official eastern gate. In consequence I was now having to face all these questions.

Hartley looked at me closely.

'How do explain the feather stuck in the dashboard?'

'It came with the car.'

'I see.'

'Anyway,' I added, 'I shouldn't have to explain myself to you. I thought it was supposed to be a free country.'

He smiled and shrugged apologetically.

'You're quite correct' he said. 'Ready for that tea?'

While he was busy with his preparations I glanced around the interior of the gatehouse. The layout was very similar to the one Rupert and I had shared at the western gate. In the adjoining room I could see a pair of bunk beds. There was a mirror on the wall and I suddenly realised I was still wearing my beach robe.

'By the way,' I said. 'I'm not a sunbather. This was the only garment available.'

'Could be worse,' said the gatekeeper. 'A few weeks ago you might have been picked up by a patrol. There were a lot of people mistaken for sunbathers during the round up.'

'Really?'

'Most unfortunate.'

'Yes, so I imagine.'

'It's all over now though. A complete change in emphasis.'

He served the tea and for a while we sat at the table in silence.

'Tell you what,' he said at length. 'We've got several spare uniforms in the back room. They're surplus to requirements. I can let you borrow one for the time being if you wish.'

'Oh, OK,' I said. 'Thanks.'

'Quite a few members of staff have left the service just lately. Disillusioned with the revised policy I dare say.'

He went and fetched several flat cardboard packages and we spent a few minutes trying to find the uniform that fitted me best. After I'd changed into my new outfit I was uncertain what to do with the beach robe.

'I'll put it through the wash,' he said. 'You might need it in future.'

'That's very kind of you.'

'Think nothing of it.' He smiled again. 'Incidentally, we're going to have to impound the black sedan.'

'What!'

'Can't be helped.'

'But it doesn't belong to me!'

'That's why we have to impound it.'

4

The procedure for handing over the black sedan was quite straightforward. Accompanied by Hartley I drove it into a nearby compound where several other cars were already being held. He gave me a receipt in exchange for the keys and asked me to sign a copy. We then returned to the gatehouse and he resumed leafing through the picture book. He told me he'd been assured by his superiors that certain species of non-native fauna were at large in the national park but as yet there were no confirmed sightings. Seemingly he viewed this last fact with some concern. He'd heard rumours that if there weren't any results very soon then the entire park authority might be disbanded.

'We've got the resources,' he declared with dismay, 'but they're all going to waste at present.'

He made no mention of Lee Montana but even so I felt my usual pang of guilt. It was my fault that she and her roving menagerie were being sought so relentlessly. If only I'd kept quiet they'd still be free to roam the British Isles unhindered. Instead their fate was in the balance. It all depended on the efficiency (or otherwise) of the park authority. The rumours about a possible disbandment were encouraging but clearly I couldn't share my sentiments with Hartley. Instead I offered a vague pronouncement.

'Perhaps there'll be more success when the weather breaks.'

'Yes, perhaps,' he said, glancing towards the window, 'but that's unlikely in the near future.'

Outside we could hear the noise of a vehicle approaching. Next moment a park authority van drew up and hooted its horn. The gate was still closed so Hartley rose from the table to go and open it.

'Don't you leave it open as a matter of course?' I asked.

'Not any more,' he replied. 'New regulations.'

'Need any help?'

'No, thanks, but come and say 'hello' anyway.'

I trailed behind him as he greeted the occupants of the van. Three uniformed men sat side-by-side in the front seat.

'There's been a sighting over by the river,' said the driver. 'We're going to try and confirm it.'

'Do you want to take an extra man with you?' said Hartley with a nod in my direction.

'By all means,' came the reply. 'The more confirmations the better.'

He released a catch and the rear door of the van swung open. Inside were another six uniformed men squeezed together on wooden benches. They somehow made room for me and the door was shut again. As we moved away I heard the driver saying goodbye to Hartley. The other men were friendly enough but didn't speak to me much. Apparently they were all impatient to get to their destination and confirm the sighting. I couldn't quite work out why this required ten men but then again the methods of the park authority had always been incomprehensible. I decided there was no harm in going along for the ride.

The road was in the usual poor condition and the van bumped and swayed along for another twenty minutes before coming to a halt.

'Here we are,' said a voice up front.

We all tumbled out.

The van had stopped in a lay-by at the curve of a sluggish river. The water was low with mud either side flanked by stone walls. A couple of slipways ran down from long wooden sheds on the opposite bank. Between the sheds were rows and rows of upturned boats with oars stacked in racks nearby.

'Tide's out,' observed the driver.

One of his companions had already clambered over the wall and descended an iron ladder that took him directly onto the mud. The other men watched from above as he examined a trail of large hoof prints that ranged along the water's edge.

'They've definitely been here,' he called. 'Fording the river perhaps.'

I noticed there were no corresponding prints on the opposite side. Furthermore there was no proper indication as to where the trail began. As far as I could tell it just seemed to be limited to a localised stretch of mud. I would have liked to go down the ladder for a closer look myself but such a move would have been highly presumptuous and risked causing resentment amongst the other men. After all, I was only a newcomer who'd been allowed to tag along with them. They appeared convinced they'd discovered genuine hoof prints in the mud and who was I to argue? As soon as the tide came in all the evidence would be washed away. In the meantime they commended one another on the veracity of their 'sighting'.

A log book was produced from the van and we were all asked to sign an entry that stated we'd witnessed the trail of hoof prints. We then resumed our journey. The plan as I understood it was to return to the eastern gate via a slightly different route. A short while later we passed a large advertising hoarding lying flat at the side of the road. In my eyes it had plainly been blown down in a gale. Nevertheless the cause of damage was recorded in the log book as destruction by 'non-native fauna'. It occurred to me that this was the second time in a day that I'd heard the same expression. I started to doubt whether it was merely a coincidence.

A much more pressing concern was my immediate future. By now I'd realised that the guys in the van assumed I was Hartley's assistant. I could hardly blame them for their error. It was an established custom that the ceremonial gates were each allocated two gatekeepers and I'd actually been rather surprised to find him working alone. When he suggested I accompanied them to the river they obviously thought I was a 'new boy' who would benefit from the experience. Now they were returning me to the eastern gate with the clear intention of dropping me off. In my current situation it was difficult to think of any alternative but really it all depended on Hartley. If he sent me on my way I'd simply have to accept the fact and get along as best I could.

It swiftly transpired that I needn't have worried. The gatehouse door was open when we arrived and Hartley was standing in the doorway waiting to welcome me back. I got out and said goodbye to the others. He let the van through the gate and with a hoot of its horn it was gone.

'You'll be a bit stuck without your wheels, won't you?' he remarked. 'How about staying around to help me for a while?'

'Well, if you're sure it's okay.'

'Of course,' he said. 'There's a spare bunk in the guest room you can use if you wish.'

'Oh, right.'

'Now let's see about some supper.'

He opened the pantry door and his face fell.

'Damn,' he said. 'I never thought of that.'

'What's up?' I asked.

'The cupboard's almost bare.'

'Ah.'

'I'm afraid we'll be on half rations for a day or two.'

'Not a problem,' I said. 'There are some lunchboxes in the black sedan. I can go and get them if you let me have the keys.'

Without hesitation he handed them over and I walked across to the compound. The thought crossed my mind that if I wanted to I could now simply jump into the car and drive away. It would have been unforgivable, however, to betray the trust Hartley was showing me so I dismissed the idea instantly. I unlocked the boot and selected two lunchboxes before locking it again.

At the very rear of the compound was a second black sedan. The other vehicles were packed tightly around so I couldn't get close enough to examine it properly. All the same it looked slightly familiar.

I returned to the gatehouse and presented Hartley with the lunchboxes.

'These are legitimate are they?' he enquired. 'I have to be certain, you understand, because technically they're in my safekeeping.'

'They're all above board,' I assured him. 'As a matter of fact they were intended for public distribution.'

'That's good.'

Now I had a question of my own.

'You know the other black sedan in the compound?'

'Yes.'

'Any idea where it came from?'

Hartley furrowed his brow.

'Bit of a conundrum actually,' he said. 'A foot patrol discovered it parked at the roadside somewhere in the midland counties. The driver said he was waiting for somebody but because he had a slight tan they mistook him for a sunbather. The car was impounded and he was led away to be interned.'

'Rather severe,' I remarked. 'Was this before the change in policy?'

'Correct,' said Hartley. 'When he was finally released they offered him a job here as my assistant. I suppose it was meant to be a sort of recompense for the inconvenience. Nice fellow but he kept himself very much to himself. Turned out he'd been given the car by an acquaintance. For some reason, though, he never tried to claim it back. He was only here for a few weeks and then suddenly he vanished. As I said before: a bit of a conundrum.'

While I was absorbing all this information I busied myself opening my lunchbox. Hartley opened his and he was visibly impressed by the contents.

'Looks as though they've been put together by a qualified nutritionist,' he said. 'Delicious too.'

I was about to mention that there were plenty more boxes in the back of the car but after second thoughts I decided against it. It was better, I reasoned, to try and keep something in reserve for the time being. Seemingly I was now *de facto* assistant gatekeeper which meant I would at least have a bed for the night. There was no suggestion, however, that the tenure would last more than a day or two. It was hardly an official appointment: I was just helping out on a temporary basis. Moreover, there was a chance that Hartley's proper assistant might reappear at any moment and displace me. I was beginning to suspect I knew exactly who he was though obviously I couldn't be certain. Why he'd gone missing was anybody's guess. No doubt he'd resurface in due course and all would be explained.

Meanwhile, Hartley wanted to hear about my expedition in the park authority van. When I gave him the details of the hoof prints and the flattened hoarding he was plainly delighted.

'That's the kind of thing we need,' he said. 'Definite proof.'

From my point of view the so-called 'sightings' were good news. I knew for a fact that Lee Montana and her roving menagerie were at least a hundred miles away in the midland counties. If it was generally believed that she was here in the east then her independence was secure for a little longer. Even so, I was alarmed by the latest developments. From what I could gather the entire resources of the park authority were being deployed in search of an elephant, some ostriches, some zebras and a young giraffe. The campaign was obviously gaining momentum and in reality it would only be a matter of time before it yielded results.

'They'll most probably send the van out again tomorrow,' said Hartley. 'You can go with them if you wish.'

'Oh, okay.'

'The more confirmations the better.'

It had been a long day and when I remembered I'd only got two hours sleep the previous night I suddenly felt tired.

'If you don't mind,' I said, 'I think I'll turn in now.'

Hartley directed me to the guest room and told me he'd give me a call in the morning. I clambered into my bunk, drifted rapidly into a deep sleep and didn't wake up until dawn.

Daylight was just beginning to stream through the window when I heard a faint crash in the distance. I recognised the sound at once. I lay listening intently in case I heard it again but now there was only silence. Quietly I rose from my bed and made my way outside. I had a rough idea which direction the sound had come from so I set off walking along the main road looking for a turning on the right. Soon I came to a junction opposite a disused bakery and then followed a minor road bounded on one side by spiked metal railings with a telegraph pole every fifty yards or so. I didn't have to go very far before I found what I was looking for. Lying across the road amidst a tangle of wires was a toppled pole. I examined it and found the word DEFECTIVE stamped on it in faded red paint. The timber was badly decayed. Nonetheless, a great deal of force would have been required to snap it off at the base. A marauding elephant, for example. Or even a tame one in capable hands.

I found this most disconcerting. Up until now I'd managed to assure myself that Lee Montana was many miles away in the midland counties. At the same time I was fully aware that the felling of telegraph poles was a speciality of hers. I recalled that in our final few days over at the western gate she'd become increasingly destructive as she vented her frustration. Telegraph poles were knocked down almost every night (not to mention one or two lamp posts). Eventually she'd set off in search of the independent settlement and the wave of devastation ceased. Several months had passed since then. Now suddenly there was evidence that she'd arrived in the east and resumed her former ways. Most disconcerting.

None of the neighbouring poles bore the red DEFECTIVE stamp: therefore I surmised that she'd been fastidious in her choice. I studied the paving slabs and the road surface for hoof prints but of course there were none. Nearby, however, was a municipal bowling green (closed). I peered through the entrance and saw a trail of trampled grass across an unkempt lawn. There was an exit at the far side where the trail abruptly ended. With nothing more to see I headed back towards the gatehouse. I'd just arrived at the junction opposite the bakery when a park authority van came along the main road and stopped beside me. It was the same team of men from the day before.

'Morning,' said the driver. 'Seen anything of interest?'

'Yes,' I replied. 'Highly interesting I would say.'

I directed him up the side road and told him I'd follow on foot. By the time I reached the fallen pole the men were swarming all over the place, taking notes and recording various facts in their log book. The driver congratulated me on my find and urged me to join their expedition.

'Actually,' I said, 'I thought I'd have some breakfast first.'

'But we're setting off straightaway.'

'Alright, well, I'll have to give it a miss then.'

He gave me a penetrating look.

'Don't you want to be a witness?' he enquired.

'Yes, but…'

'Doesn't sound like it.'

'No, really, I do.'

By now some of the other men had gathered around us. They appeared baffled that I was reluctant to go with them.

'You're letting the side down,' remarked one of them.

'Sorry,' I said, 'but I haven't had my breakfast yet. I expect you've already had yours.'

'That's got nothing to do with it.'

With a shake of his head he turned and got back into the van. There was some murmuring and then his companions followed. Last to join them was the driver. He slid behind the wheel and gave me another penetrating look before starting the engine and moving away.

5

Hartley was rather displeased that I'd wandered off on my own.

'I was just down the road,' I explained. 'Having a look around.'

'Well, you've missed the van,' he said. 'I was under the impression you wanted to go with them. You can't keep letting people down you know.'

I tried to mollify him by offering to fetch a couple of lunchboxes for breakfast. Unfortunately the gesture backfired.

'Oh, yes, I've been thinking about those lunchboxes,' he announced. 'I went over to the compound a while ago and discovered there are dozens of them hidden in the black sedan.'

'Yes, there are,' I admitted.

'Technically they're in my safekeeping so you'd better put them all in the pantry for the time being.'

He was on the verge of handing me the car keys but then he seemed to change his mind.

'I'll come with you,' he said.

The lunchboxes were stored in a hamper. It would have made sense to carry it across to the gatehouse and empty it there but instead Hartley insisted we took only the lunchboxes. For this reason we had to make several journeys carrying half a dozen each. The task took about a quarter of an hour to complete and during that time I got the odd feeling we were being watched from somewhere nearby. I glanced around once or twice but saw nobody. When we'd finished we went inside for breakfast.

'Half rations I'm afraid,' said Hartley. 'Supplies are very low at the moment.'

'Why don't we just open a lunchbox?' I suggested.

'Can't do that,' he replied. 'I've checked the regulations and they count as impounded goods. We shouldn't really have touched any last night.'

We sat down to a notably sparse breakfast. Apparently I was in Hartley's bad books and I concluded it was because I hadn't told him about the other lunchboxes. Or maybe he thought I was being insufficiently zealous about the search for 'non-native fauna'. I realised I needed to at least feign interest so I told him all about the fallen telegraph pole.

His mood brightened instantly.

'That's the best sort of evidence,' he said. 'As a matter of fact a similar incident occurred a couple of weeks ago. About a mile away it was. A pole came down by the old post office. That's what sparked off the search in this region.'

Hartley told me he regretted not having witnessed any of these events himself. He confessed that it was nobody's fault but his own:

he should have been more vigilant. There was a high probability that non-native fauna had passed close by the gatehouse without him even noticing. Such negligence was unforgivable. Nevertheless, the recent reports had brought hope that all was not lost.

'The more confirmations the better,' he declared.

During that first morning I discovered how much had changed since my time as a gatekeeper over in the west. In those days the majority of British people had shown little interest in visiting the national park and preferred to stay on the coast and sunbathe. It was widely known that anybody who ventured into the hinterland beyond the gate would find nothing but dereliction, abandonment and encroaching wilderness. The roads were full of potholes, travellers were infrequent and their destinations obscure. As a source of recreation the park was not generally recommended. I was surprised, therefore, when only half an hour after we'd finished breakfast a car pulled up at the eastern gate. Hartley went out to greet the new arrivals and I followed close behind. The car was a vintage model: one of the few types for which spare parts were still available. There were two men in the front and three women in the back, all fairly young, all smiling and all with their windows wound down.

'We're trying to get to the river,' said the driver. 'Is this the right road?'

'Yes it is,' said Hartley. 'Keep going straight for about ten miles and then take the left fork.'

'Thanks.'

'Let us know if you spot anything interesting.'

I opened the gate to allow the car through and again I got the feeling I was being watched from somewhere nearby. I didn't have time to investigate further, however, because a minute later another car appeared. And then another after that. They were all heading for the river and I began to suspect that word must have spread about the 'sighting' of the previous day. As the morning wore on yet more vehicles passed by, many of them seemingly on the verge of obsolescence. Hartley insisted on adhering to the regulations which meant I was constantly opening and closing the gate. This gave me the opportunity to question some of the occupants to find out how much they actually knew. I adopted a casual manner and innocently enquired why the river had become so attractive all of a sudden. The answers they gave suggested somebody had seriously misled them. They were aware that an elephant, some zebras, some ostriches and a young giraffe were roaming free in the British Isles and they wanted to help locate them. Clearly they had no idea of the park authority's ultimate intention. Thankfully there was no mention of Lee Montana so I assumed that for the moment she remained out of the picture. All the same I was rather disturbed by the influx of all these incomers. Every car was full of eager young people keen to get to the river and help (or at least seen to be helping). None of them appeared properly equipped for any kind of 'search and rescue' mission: they were more like day trippers embarking on an excursion. Moreover, a lot of the cars looked as though they would only just be capable of completing the journey. As the latest batch departed Hartley turned to me.

'Well,' he said, 'I imagine we'll soon receive some positive results.'

'Yes, maybe.'

'How would you like to pop in and make some tea?'

'Alright.'

While I was engaged in the kitchen I heard yet another vehicle approaching the gate. I decided to let Hartley deal with it and continued with my task. Once the kettle had boiled and I'd stirred the tea I went back outside to let him know it was ready. The vehicle was just leaving and to my surprise I saw that it was the glasshouse on wheels we'd passed back in the midland counties. Hartley closed the gate behind it and came over to join me.

'It's a research vehicle,' he announced, 'or so the driver told me.'

'Researching what?' I enquired.

'He didn't say.'

We watched as it trundled sedately away and headed into the park, then we went and had our tea. After that the traffic eased off and for the time being we were able to relax.

'As it's quiet,' I said at length, 'is it okay if I go for another walk? Just to get my bearings.'

'Alright,' said Hartley. 'Why don't you have a look at that felled pole over by the old post office?'

'Yes, I think I will.'

He gave me directions and I set off eastward along the main road seeking a turning on the left. He'd mentioned the post office was a mile away but actually it was less than that. I got there easily in a quarter of an hour and soon spotted the pole lying across the road amidst the usual tangle of wires. I was just examining it for the telltale red DEFECTIVE stamp when I was startled by a voice behind me.

'An obvious target for sabotage.'

I turned around and saw Rupert. Where he'd appeared from I had no idea but I guessed he'd been tracking my movements. He was wearing a park authority uniform that looked a little worse for wear.

I nodded towards the fallen pole.

'So this was your work, was it?' I asked.

'Correct,' he replied. 'It's remarkable what can be achieved with a hook, a rope and a pulley block.'

We shook hands and he beckoned me to follow him. He led me round behind the post office and up a fire escape to an adjoining building. A fire door had been propped open and inside was a room with windows like portholes. The layout was decidedly austere.

'My operational headquarters,' said Rupert. 'I've been based here for a few weeks now.'

'So I suppose we can thank you for the trail of trampled grass?'

'Yes.'

'What about the hoof prints by the river?'

'Easily done with a little imagination.'

I informed him that as far as I knew Lee Montana and her roving menagerie were still somewhere in the midland counties.

'I presume,' I said, 'that you're attempting to draw the search away from her.'

'That's the plan,' he replied, 'but I think I've been a little bit too successful.'

'Oh, yes?'

'The trouble is the general public have got involved. You'll have seen them coming through the gate in their hordes. They all believe they're helping in the search but very soon they're going to overrun the entire park.'

'So there'll be nowhere to hide.'

'Quite.'

Rupert seemed acutely concerned and I had to admit I was impressed by the lengths he'd gone to on behalf of Lee Montana. I needed to return to my duties fairly soon so he told me he'd keep in touch.

'By the way,' he said, 'I noticed you arrived in Ambrose's black sedan.'

'Yes.'

'How is he?'

'Not sure, really. I haven't seen him for a while.'

We parted and I made my way back towards the gatehouse. As I walked I checked each telegraph pole I passed to see if any of them bore a red DEFECTIVE stamp. There were three in total: three potential targets for Rupert's sabotage campaign. (The exercise was purely academic, of course. I knew from our previous association that Rupert was very thorough in his methods. He was bound to have studied the area already and taken note of the three poles. Whether his next strike would be here or further afield was less certain. Ultimately it depended on how the situation developed.)

When finally I approached the gatehouse I saw that a park authority van had pulled up outside. All of its windows were open and Hartley was standing beside it deep in conversation with the occupants. After my last encounter with the guys from the park authority my initial inclination was to try to avoid them. With a job like mine, however, I realised this was impossible so I sauntered up to the van and gave the driver a friendly nod. He nodded in return but said nothing.

Hartley was in a buoyant mood.

'Good news,' he announced. 'There's been another confirmed sighting.'

'Great,' I said, trying to sound enthusiastic. 'More hoof prints?'

'Better than that,' he said. 'They spotted a girl riding on an elephant.'

'But they can't have!'

I regretted my outburst immediately. It brought a chorus of indignation from inside the van and the driver jabbed his finger at me through the window.

'You're a bit of a doubting Thomas, aren't you?' he snapped. 'We know what we saw.'

Still reeling from the news I turned and headed into the gatehouse. I heard the van move away and a moment later Hartley came in and slammed the door behind him. He was plainly annoyed.

'Don't you believe she's out there?' he demanded.

'Of course,' I replied.

'Well, you'd better pull your socks up. Otherwise I'll have to find myself another assistant.'

'Sorry.'

Following this episode I adopted my former policy of keeping my reservations to myself. Luckily we were quite busy so there was no time for further recriminations from Hartley. Many of the vehicles that had entered the park during the morning were returning to the coast, though there now seemed to be fewer of them. An explanation was soon forthcoming when a car arrived at the gate carrying seven people. They were all jammed together and sounded as if they were having enormous fun.

'We broke down,' laughed a woman in the back seat. 'Had to abandon our car by the river.'

'Sorry to hear that,' I said. 'Was it due to the shortage of spare parts?'

'Yes, but it doesn't matter,' she replied. 'We saw the girl on the elephant and that's all that counts.'

Hartley was standing nearby when she uttered these words and he now gave me a triumphant look. As the car continued its journey he clapped his hands together and went into the gatehouse.

All through the afternoon I heard similar reports. In every case the people in the car had caught a distant glimpse of a girl on an elephant. When I enquired whether she was travelling alone, however, the accounts varied. Sometimes she was accompanied by a zebra, an ostrich and a young giraffe; sometimes by half a dozen zebras; sometimes it was just the giraffe (age unspecified). I found this inconsistency quite encouraging. By now I was coming to the conclusion that these so-called witnesses were somehow deluding themselves about what they'd actually seen. Nonetheless they must have got the idea from somewhere in the first place: otherwise they wouldn't have descended on the park in such numbers.

Meanwhile there were several more instances of carloads of people rescuing other carloads. The list of catastrophes ranged from collapsed suspension to overheated engines to simply running out of fuel. The common element was that the problems had all occurred whilst in pursuit of the elusive menagerie. As each overloaded vehicle passed through the gate I heard yet more tales of 'near sightings', 'possible sightings' and 'confirmed sightings'. The occupants of the cars were jubilant about the part they'd played in the search. Their losses, apparently, were inconsequential.

Quite late in the day another park authority van pulled up outside the gatehouse. By now I was expecting to be confronted at any moment by a squad of indoctrinated ruffians. I could tell from Hartley's demeanour that I was generally regarded as a dissident and therefore I braced myself for trouble.

I was surprised, then, to see that the driver was all alone. I recognised him at once. It was Davy: the man who'd overseen my release from internment. He was evidently surprised as well.

'Oh, hello,' he said, through his window. 'What are you doing in uniform?'

'I'm helping out temporarily,' I replied. 'Hartley needed an assistant.'

Davy got out of the van and went round to open the back doors.

'I've brought your fresh supplies,' he announced.

The vehicle was laden with hundreds of lunchboxes. Hartley emerged from the gatehouse and began taking a proprietorial interest in the shipment. He signed for six boxes and carried them inside. I waited until he'd gone before turning to Davy.

'How's Brock?' I enquired. 'Last time I saw him he was heading for solitary confinement.'

'All rather embarrassing actually,' said Davy. 'He escaped from the stadium within twenty-four hours.'

'Ah.'

'My fault I'm afraid. I accidentally left the double doors open. That's why I've been demoted to delivery man.'

'Where's your next drop?'

'The western gate. I'll be travelling overnight.'

After Davy had departed I went into the gatehouse to join Hartley. He was contemplating the six lunchboxes stacked on the table.

'Quite handy,' he said at length. 'They're identical to the ones that were impounded.'

I knew from experience that the contents were inferior but I passed no comment and merely nodded in agreement.

'It means we can replace the two we opened yesterday evening,' he continued, 'to keep the books balanced.'

'Won't that leave us short again?' I enquired.

'I'm afraid so.'

As Hartley rearranged the pantry I reflected on his strict adhesion to rules and regulations. By setting aside two of the new lunchboxes he was effectively putting us back on half rations: this amounted to self-sacrifice of the highest order. He was plainly incorruptible, immune to sharp practises and certainly not the kind whose sole concern was going home early on a Friday (as a matter of fact the gatehouse was his home). His loyalty to the park authority was beyond question to the extent that he viewed the possibility of disbandment as a personal slight.

Moreover, he acquiesced in whatever policy was being pursued at any particular time: hence his acceptance without question of the recent sightings.

For all his diligence, however, I knew that Hartley would get no thanks. Over the next few days our workload became steadily heavier. An increasing volume of traffic passed through the gate as more and more people joined the search yet we received no word from the park authority. There was no sense of any proper oversight amongst our superiors: nobody collating all the information we gathered and nobody offering guidance. We were simply left alone to cope as best we could. Members of the public clearly thought it was their duty to inform us of what they'd seen and as a consequence we were practically besieged in our gatehouse. Many were now identifying themselves as 'confirmed witnesses' and wanted to know where they should register. It transpired that there were notices along the coast instructing them to do this but unfortunately Hartley and I had no answers. Further problems arose with cars breaking down inside the park. Many of these vehicles had been out of use for long periods and just weren't up to the task. Accordingly we heard frequent reports of travellers being stranded. There were also those who'd decided to return to the park on a permanent basis. For these pioneering types it was a one way journey as they sought to settle and begin a new life in the interior. Seemingly, though, few of them had made any long term provision for the future. To judge from their enthusiastic talk they believed that the search was an end in itself. They thought they only had to catch sight of the girl on the elephant and everything else would fall naturally into place.

Yet actually the opposite was true: by the end of the week the park had descended into disarray.

6

Just before dawn one morning I was woken by the sound of an aircraft flying low overhead. I could hear propellers whirring and guessed it was some sort of transport plane. After it had gone I lay listening for further noises from outside but apart from the usual birdsong all else was quiet. There wasn't even the distant crash of a falling telegraph pole. (The crashes had ceased since my meeting with Rupert and I assumed he'd suspended operations.) I dozed for a while longer before finally deciding to get up. After I'd washed and dressed I headed for the kitchen and found a fresh pot of tea on the table. This told me Hartley was already up and about but there was no sign of him. I then noticed that the front door was open so I went and peered outside. The sight that met me was astonishing. The road, the pavement and the lay-by opposite were all littered with printed leaflets. There were leaflets in the trees and bushes and yet more scattered in nearby yards and gardens. A few were still fluttering down from the sky. Hartley had picked one up and was standing by the gate reading it.

'Morning,' I said. 'I see we've had a special delivery.'

'Yes,' he replied. 'There'll be a lot of tidying up to do.'

On one side of the leaflet was a grainy image of a girl riding an elephant through the savannah. The other side requested all confirmed witnesses to report and register immediately at the Eastbrook Stadium.

Hartley folded his leaflet and put it in his pocket before going into the gatehouse to fetch a broom.

'They've dropped far too many,' he said. 'Whatever were they thinking of?'

He didn't say precisely who 'they' were but it was obvious that this was the work of the park authority. I realised it was the first occasion I'd heard Hartley utter a critical comment about them and naturally I agreed with him. For days we'd been left in the dark and now suddenly there were all these leaflets falling from the sky. It was a perfect example of the park authority's abject profligacy. I was normally an easy-going type of person but sometimes they tested my forbearance to the limits. In my opinion they were nothing but an incompetent shower. Their shortcomings were manifold. They lacked any vision. They constantly swung from one extreme to the other. Worst of all, instead of directing their resources towards worthwhile goals they wasted them on projects that were illusory.

On a more personal level I was dismayed to see all these leaflets depicting Lee Montana. It meant that the hunt had intensified and she would need to be increasingly vigilant if she wished to maintain her freedom. My only consolation was that her pursuers were patently on the wrong trail.

It goes without saying that Hartley's attempt to sweep up all the leaflets was doomed to failure. There were probably thousands of them spread right across the region. Maybe even millions. Even so, I knew he wouldn't rest until the area around the gatehouse was presentable. Appearances were paramount for Hartley: therefore I simply let him get on with it. Meanwhile I went inside and had a cup of tea. When at last he joined me in the kitchen he had a piece of good news.

'Should be getting some more supplies today,' he announced. 'Then we'll be back on full rations.'

This at least was a mercy.

'Do you know where the Eastbrook Stadium is?' I enquired.

'Of course,' said Hartley. 'It's about four miles away.'

'Will you be going to register?'

'I can't really.'

'Why?'

'I'm not a confirmed witness.'

'But you would if you could?'

'Unquestionably.'

Hartley seemed rather disappointed that he was so close to the action yet unable to play a part in it. I realised I had an advantage over him because actually I was a genuine confirmed witness. I judged, however, that it would be unwise to mention the fact. Instead I pondered how his situation might be rectified. Obviously my thoughts were bound to be interrupted because traffic passing through the gate was already beginning to build up. Nevertheless as the hours went by I gradually formulated a plan of action. Its success would ultimately depend on Rupert but I was sure I could rely on him.

Throughout the morning a stream of vehicles headed into the park (few of them ever to return). I also noticed that increasing numbers of people were travelling by bicycle or on foot. Many of these individuals were tanned and healthy-looking but I doubted if they classified themselves as sunbathers. By contrast, they constituted an entirely different breed whose only desire was to join the ranks of confirmed witnesses. Amongst those cycling past was a woman who bore a close resemblance to Gemma from the independent settlement. Unfortunately, I missed the opportunity to speak to her because at the time I was busy giving directions to a car.

Around midday there was a slight lull in the traffic so I told Hartley I was going for a short stroll. I wandered along the main road in a westerly direction and after about two hundred yards I spotted a telegraph pole with a red DEFECTIVE stamp on it. This was perfect for my requirements. Swiftly, I attached a note to the pole briefly explaining Hartley's predicament. I knew that Rupert kept the gatehouse under observation and I was confident he would take appropriate action.

When I resumed work in the afternoon I began thinking about Gemma again. I was convinced it was her I'd seen cycling into the park and I regretted not having made more effort to catch her attention when she'd been so close. Obviously it was too late now. For a while I told myself there was a chance she'd return by the same route later in the day. In truth, though, this was unlikely. I'd learned from our past encounters that Gemma was a fervent trailblazer. She'd been amongst the first arrivals at the independent settlement and I imagined she was now seeking a similar refuge. Turning back would be unthinkable for a woman of her calibre so I tried my best to put her out of my mind.

Just before dusk a park authority van pulled up at the gate. It was Davy with the new supplies. He looked thoroughly harassed.

'The roads are getting crowded,' he said. 'I haven't seen them so busy since before the purchase.'

He handed over six lunchboxes and Hartley signed the receipt.

'Next stop the western gate?' I asked.

'I'll be heading there eventually,' said Davy, 'but I've got to call in at the Eastbrook Stadium first. Apparently there's been a problem with the registration process and a few people have had to be detained overnight.'

'I suppose they'll all need feeding,' remarked Hartley.

'Quite.'

During the afternoon a desultory breeze had been stirring in the treetops. There were still a few leaflets trapped amidst the branches and now one of them came floating down. Davy caught it and examined it distractedly. He spent several seconds peering at the grainy image of a girl on an elephant then suddenly glanced up at me.

'Didn't you catch sight of her a few months ago?'

'Yes,' I acknowledged.

The revelation caused Hartley to start in surprise.

'You didn't tell me,' he said.

'I didn't know I had to.'

'But we've been living under the same roof for a week!' he protested. 'We're all meant to be on the lookout for confirmed sightings. What was the point of keeping quiet about it?'

'Well, it wasn't around here that I saw her,' I said weakly. 'It was near the western gate.'

'Oh, yes,' said Davy. 'I remember now. You were a gatekeeper over there, weren't you?'

'Yes.'

'You didn't tell me that either,' said Hartley.

He regarded me with a sombre expression as if he thought I'd betrayed him. Davy didn't appear particularly friendly either and I realised I was in a bit of a corner. I wanted to explain to them that I disagreed with the park authority's latest strategy but I was uncertain of the reception I'd receive. I knew for sure that Hartley was a devotedly loyal employee who would be affronted by such views. Davy, on the other hand, was less easy to fathom. I'd seen from my earlier dealings with him that he was a conscientious man who did his job properly. Whether he truly believed in the precepts of the park authority was a different question altogether. Under the circumstances I decided my best option was to play the innocent.

'What do you think I should do?'

'The answer's obvious,' said Hartley. 'Go along to the stadium and register.'

'Alright,' I replied. 'I will when I've got time.'

'It says 'immediately' on the leaflet.'

'You mean tonight?'

'Of course.'

'You could come with me in the van,' said Davy.

'But didn't you mention they were detaining people?'

'That's a risk you'd have to take.'

I considered his offer for a few moments.

'No, thanks all the same,' I said at length, 'but I'll leave it until tomorrow if you don't mind. I can't see a few hours making any difference now.'

'Okay.'

Davy started his engine and waved us both goodbye before continuing his journey. Hartley was clearly unhappy with my decision but he voiced no further objections. Instead he went into the gatehouse and began preparing supper. I followed him inside.

'Our first taste of full rations,' I said. 'Don't want to miss out on that, do I?'

My attempt at lightheartedness fell on deaf ears: Hartley was having none of it. We shared supper in silence and for the remainder of the evening he made a point of ignoring me, only communicating when it was entirely necessary and finally retiring to bed without a word. I headed for my bunk in the spare room wondering how I could make amends. There was a chance that a trip to the Eastbrook Stadium could restore relations to a satisfactory level but actually I was quite wary of going there. What bothered me most was the possibility of being detained. I'd already been interned once and I had no wish to repeat the experience. Having said that, however, I also knew it would be difficult to wriggle out of my commitment. I'd informed both Hartley and Davy that I would go and register tomorrow so I really felt I had no alternative.

7

I was woken at dawn by the sound of something crashing down. (I estimated the distance to be about two hundred yards away.) Immediately I got up and padded barefoot to the kitchen. Hartley had just finished making a pot of tea. Now he was standing by the window with his head cocked and listening intently.

'Did you hear that?' he said. 'Seemed fairly close by.'

He had an expectant look about him as if a long-awaited moment had finally arrived.

'Why don't you go and investigate?' I suggested. 'This might be your chance to be a witness.'

'Yes, it might, mightn't it?'

'I'll attend to the gate.'

'Righto.'

Hartley had apparently forgotten that he was meant to be giving me the cold shoulder. He put his boots on and hurried out into the chilly morning air. Meanwhile I washed and dressed before returning to the kitchen for a light breakfast. Fortunately there was no traffic as yet so I was able to take my time. I was on my second cup of tea when he returned. He was evidently overjoyed.

'There's a telegraph pole down in the road,' he announced. 'Hoof prints all over the place and a nearby fence flattened.'

'Did you see the girl on the elephant?' I enquired.

'I think I caught a glimpse of her in the distance.'

'Perfect,' I said. 'You've got your first confirmed sighting.'

I offered him some tea.

'Not for the moment, thanks,' he said. 'That fallen pole's blocking the road. We need to get it moved fairly soon.'

'Shall I come and help?'

'Yes, please.'

'What about the gate?'

'We'll have to leave it open.'

We arrived at the fallen pole a few minutes later and surveyed the damage. I had to confess that Rupert had made an excellent job of it. Quite authentic actually. There were hoof prints on the grass verge and beyond the smashed fence was a trail of trampled undergrowth. Hartley pointed towards the place where he'd supposedly spotted the girl on the elephant. All I could see was a cement mixer in an overgrown builder's yard but I passed no comment.

The pole itself proved impossible to move. No matter how much we shoved and pushed we just couldn't budge it. We were standing amidst a tangle of wires trying to work out what to do when a car came along from the east. It slowed down to pass through the gateway and then continued on to where we stood. There were two men in the front and two in the back. As soon as they saw the fallen pole they were all out of the car in an instant.

'Must be a confirmed sighting, right?' said the driver.

'Yes,' said Hartley. 'Just a short while ago.'

'That's good. The more the better.'

The four men examined the area knowingly. They produced notebooks and wrote down various details of the incident. I noticed they were all wearing T-shirts emblazoned with the letters: CW

'Had any luck yourselves?' I asked.

'We certainly have,' came the reply. 'As a matter of fact we're on our way to register now.'

'Trouble is the road's blocked.'

'No problem. We'll have it cleared in a jiffy.'

With the help of an extra four pairs of hands we got the pole moved fairly easily. Once we'd manhandled it onto the verge the driver turned to Hartley and me.

'So,' he said, 'who made the sighting?'

'Me,' said Hartley.

'Well, do you want to come with us and register your claim?'

'Oh, I don't know about that.'

'Why?'

'I'm not allowed to leave my post without permission.'

'But you're supposed to register immediately,' I pointed out, 'and anyway I can look after the gate during your absence.'

Despite his elation at becoming a confirmed witness Hartley remained anxious. It even concerned him that we'd left the gate open (even though we could see it clearly from where we were). He was undoubtedly a slave of duty but in my opinion he was taking it too far. Finally the driver interjected.

'Registration won't take long,' he said brightly, 'and then we can bring you back.'

Thus reassured, Hartley at last agreed to go with them. He squeezed into the car with the others and a minute later they were gone. I waved goodbye and wandered back to the gate.

A trickle of traffic had started to come through but for the moment the workload was light. The weather was warming up again so I sat down on a bench in front of the gatehouse and basked in the early morning sunshine. I calculated that Hartley would be gone for an hour at the most. In the meantime I decided there would be no harm in leaving the gate open as long as I kept an eye on it. For one precious hour I was in sole charge and I intended to take it easy. That was the plan anyway.

As it transpired there would be little opportunity for lounging around. As the morning passed the trickle gradually became a stream which in turn transformed into a torrent. After that I was constantly on my feet. The gate may have been wide open but nonetheless there was soon a perpetual queue of motorists stopping to make enquiries. Mostly they wanted to know where was the best place to go to get a sight of the girl on the elephant. In response I gave directions that sounded highly detailed but were actually rather vague. The more discerning travellers had gone to the trouble to learn the migratory habits of elephants, ostriches, zebras and giraffes. They were aware that Great Britain was a former industrialised country with only limited access to grazing and fresh water. Therefore their questions were more specific. Some were in search of arable lands, pastures, orchards and forests; others sought rivers, lakes, reservoirs, canals and even millponds. What all of them had in common (whether they were discerning or not) was their yearning to be counted as a confirmed witness. I got so involved guiding these hopeful souls on their journey that I completely lost track of time. It was only when I started to feel peckish that I realised it was well after midday. There was still no sign of Hartley and I guessed that the registration process must have been slower than anticipated. During a brief lull around one o'clock I managed to grab a lunchbox from the pantry. Very shortly, however, it was back to work again. All afternoon the onslaught continued and not until the light was beginning to fail did the flow of traffic finally subside. After closing the gate I went indoors and sat down for a well-earned rest.

I must have dozed off because the next thing I knew there was a horn honking outside. I peered through the window and saw the car containing the four men. Hartley wasn't with them so I dashed out to see what had happened.

'I'm afraid he's been temporarily detained,' explained the driver. 'Bit of a problem with his registration.'

'What sort of problem?' I asked.

'Insufficient enthusiasm by all accounts.'

Needless to say I was shocked by the news. From what I'd seen of Hartley he was a model of enthusiasm. He'd been as keen as anyone to get a confirmed sighting of the girl on the elephant but now it seemed he'd had it thrown back in his face.

'By the way,' continued the driver, 'I gather you're a confirmed witness yourself.'

'Yes, I am.'

'Then maybe it's time you went and registered as well.'

I heard a murmur of assent from within the car. Plainly his three companions concurred.

'Well, actually,' I said, 'I was supposed to go today but Hartley went instead.'

'So you'll go tomorrow, will you?'

'Probably, yes.'

'Alright, bye.'

'Bye.'

As the car departed I noticed there was an enamel badge fixed to the rear bumper displaying the letters: CW

When I got back inside the gatehouse I pondered whether or not I should simply abandon the place and move on. It was a very tempting option. The keys from all the impounded vehicles were hanging on a rack on the wall so I'd have easy access to the black sedan. At the same time I could reclaim ownership of a few lunchboxes. I would then be free to return to the midland counties and try to find Lee Montana. She urgently needed to be apprised of the situation. I was the only person who knew the true intentions of the park authority and I felt obliged to warn her.

On close consideration, though, I realised I couldn't just desert Hartley when he was in a spot of bother. He'd been good enough to offer me accommodation when otherwise I'd have been stranded: the least I could do was look after the gatehouse in his absence. Besides, he might return at any moment. Just because the four guys in the car said he'd been detained it didn't necessarily mean he was under lock and key. All their talk about 'insufficient enthusiasm' may have merely been their misinterpretation of an administrative glitch.

Furthermore, my chances of making contact with Lee Montana were practically nil. I'd tried once before and failed and since then the odds against success had become much greater. I couldn't even be certain if she was still in the midland counties. For all I knew she might be anywhere in the British Isles by now. I also needed to accept that she probably wouldn't welcome my help anyway. She had long experience of evading search parties and she'd proved herself quite capable. All the same, life on the run was bound to be taking its toll. By joining in the search I would only add to her difficulties rather than reduce them.

Lastly, of course, was the fact that the black sedan was almost out of fuel. If I set off with a low tank I'd run the risk of getting stuck in the middle of nowhere. Therefore, after much reflection, I decided to remain where I was in the hope that Hartley would come back soon.

Shortly after dark I received a visit from Rupert. I updated him on the state of play and then we sat down at the table to share a lunchbox.

'There are plenty more in the pantry,' I explained, 'but we're only allowed one at a time. Hartley's very particular with the rations.'

'I know,' said Rupert. 'He was the same when I was his assistant.'

'What do you do for supplies these days, by the way?'

'A guy called Davy drops off a few lunchboxes from time to time.'

116

'Ah, yes,' I said. 'I know Davy.'

'He was a guard during my period of internment and we've stayed in touch ever since.'

'So he's aware of your clandestine activities, is he?'

'He doesn't ask and I don't tell.'

'I see.'

'I've a feeling his sympathies diverge from the orthodox park authority line but whether he approves of my diversionary tactics is a different matter altogether.'

'He's very hard to read.'

'Yes.'

Rupert glanced around the interior of the gatehouse as if reminding himself of his former home. He studied the row of car keys hanging on the rack and he gazed through the window into the darkness outside. Finally he peered at my uniform. It still looked crisp and new whereas his was battered and worn.

'We didn't wear uniforms back at the western gate,' he remarked.

'There was no need really,' I said. 'It was all much more casual in those days.'

'Changed completely now though.'

'And not for the better either.'

For a while we reminisced about our spell as gatekeepers and how we'd been more or less free to do what we liked. We'd operated the western gate according to our personal requirements, enjoying all the perquisites of the job (which included plentiful tips and gratuities) with little or no supervision. Looking back now it seemed like an entirely different world. We both agreed about that. I'd been acquainted with Rupert long enough, however, to know that he wasn't interested in small talk. I sensed he was leading up to something and sure enough he eventually revealed his hand.

'This gate,' he said, 'is an excellent place to pick up information. All those people passing through can help to generate a composite picture of public opinion. By asking the right sort of questions we can find out who approves of the park authority and who opposes it.'

'So you want me to gather information, do you?' I asked.

'Yes, if you don't mind,' he replied, 'but you wouldn't be working on your own. I'd be here as well.'

'You mean as a gatekeeper?'

'Correct.'

'But what if Hartley comes back?'

'We'll worry about that when it happens,' said Rupert. 'Don't forget I can easily slip away at any time.'

So it was arranged that Rupert would join me on a casual basis next morning and help me with the gate for most of the day. He assured me he'd do most of the questioning; moreover he would do it in such a subtle manner that the travelling public would be completely unaware they were being probed.

'The trouble is,' I pointed out, 'most of the people coming this way believe they're predestined to be confirmed witnesses. They hardly represent the British population as a whole.'

'Maybe not quite yet,' conceded Rupert, 'but they could be in the majority very soon.'

8

During the night there was another leaflet drop. The aircraft came over just before dawn and the message it carried was emphatic:

CONFIRMED WITNESS? GET REGISTERED

Rupert arrived about eight o'clock while I was attempting to sweep up. There was a second broom in the gatehouse and the two of us had the area looking fairly tidy by the time the first vehicles appeared. We'd gathered the surplus leaflets into a pile and we now handed them to motorists as they passed through the gate. In this way Rupert was provided with a perfect excuse to briefly engage them in conversation. He only delayed each car for a minute at the most but still he was able to obtain all kinds of insights. It swiftly transpired that many were heading directly for the Eastbrook Stadium because they'd already had a confirmed sighting of the girl on the elephant. The places where she'd supposedly been spotted were sometimes many miles apart (much further than she could possibly travel in a day) yet all the witnesses were convinced their claims were genuine. After they'd registered they intended to return to these hallowed sites and create permanent settlements.

'Their belief is highly commendable,' remarked Rupert, 'but needless to say it's a case of mass deception.'

'My thoughts exactly.'

'They're being lured to the Eastbrook Stadium on false pretences.'

We were taking advantage of a temporary lull in the traffic and our discussion now turned to Hartley. Twenty-four hours had passed since his departure and still we'd received no word from him. I was partially to blame for his detainment and I felt more than a little guilty about it.

'If he hasn't come back by this evening,' I said, 'I think I'll have a stroll over to the stadium just to make sure he's okay.'

Rupert was examining one of the leaflets that had been dropped overnight.

'There's a map printed on the back,' he said. 'It's about four miles away.'

'That's not very far.'

'It'd be quicker to take the black sedan.'

'I can't really,' I said. 'It's meant to be impounded.'

Rupert gave me a penetrating look.

'Who's going to know?' he said. 'We can put it back afterwards and nobody will be the wiser.'

'So you're planning to come with me, are you?' I asked.

'I think I should, yes. Don't forget I'm also partially to blame for his detainment. Besides, we might be able to discover exactly what's going on there.'

'Suppose so.'

As the afternoon wore on and dusk approached I became increasingly doubtful that Hartley would return. As a matter of fact there was absolutely no traffic of any kind coming in the opposite direction: it was definitely a one way trip for the confirmed witnesses. I'd now started to warm to Rupert's idea of 'borrowing' the black sedan for our brief excursion to the Eastbrook Stadium. It would be perfectly alright as long as we put it back in the compound precisely where it was before. Obviously we'd need to leave the gate open during our absence but that shouldn't present a problem either. By about eight o'clock we'd had our supper and were ready to go. We took the car keys from the rack, locked up the gatehouse and headed into the night.

'Good job it's only a short journey,' I said as I started up the black sedan. 'Fuel tank's very low.'

Rupert was in charge of navigation. He directed me to continue along the main road for about two miles and then look for a turning on the left. We couldn't help noticing that the roadside was littered with abandoned vehicles. There were scores of them! Presumably they'd broken down and their owners had continued their journey to the stadium on foot.

Ever since the time of the purchase I'd been accustomed to seeing roadsigns that had either faded or succumbed to rust. Trying to travel anywhere particular had been a matter of guesswork so I was surprised when we began passing brand new signs indicating the way to the Eastbrook Stadium.

'They've only been put up recently,' observed Rupert. 'Somebody clearly means business.'

As we drew closer to our destination we started to look for somewhere to leave the black sedan. We'd agreed beforehand that it was best not to attract too much attention to ourselves so we planned to walk for the last quarter of a mile. The only trouble was that many other people had seemingly had the same idea. There were cars parked tightly together in the side streets leading to the stadium and it was only after a long search that we finally found a space.

'They haven't progressed very far, have they?' I said. 'I thought they were all supposed to be heading into the interior.'

'Maybe they've been detained,' said Rupert.

His face was obscured in the dimness of the evening so I was unable to tell whether he meant the remark to be taken seriously. His tone of voice, however, was wary. Henceforth we proceeded in silence. As we got nearer the stadium we saw pale lights flickering in the sky above, then all of a sudden we heard a familiar sound. There was music blaring from loudspeakers and we both recognised it immediately: it was the theme tune from the promotional film about Lee Montana. We could also hear the muffled commentary. As we stood listening it was easy to imagine the grainy footage of her riding an elephant through the savannah, accompanied by some zebras, some ostriches and a young giraffe. Despite the noise from the soundtrack I lowered my voice to speak to Rupert.

'I wonder how many people are in there watching that?'

'Don't know,' he replied, 'but it could be thousands.'

We moved cautiously around the circumference of the stadium. There were numerous entrances, each equipped with a set of turnstiles above which were notices that said: THIS WAY TO REGISTER

Rupert and I knew the theme tune well enough to be aware that the ten minute film was about to end. As soon as it did there came a tumult of applause from inside the stadium. We withdrew into the shadows to observe the crowds leaving. When nobody appeared we then concluded that another film was about to be shown. Perhaps there was going to be a main feature. Instead, however, after a short interval the same theme music resumed once more.

'Must be very popular,' remarked Rupert.

We remained in the shadows and waited as a further ten minutes elapsed. After the film ended there was again a burst of appreciative applause. When eventually it died down a small group of people emerged from one of the exits. They were talking excitedly to each other as they headed for a side street. Wandering along behind them was a straggler who for some reason had become separated from his companions. He paused for a moment to get his bearings and was about to follow after them when an abrupt call brought him to a halt.

'Wait there!'

Five men strode out of the exit and gathered around him. They were all wearing park authority uniforms.

Rupert and I listened attentively as they cross-examined the straggler.

'Confirmed witness, are you?'

'Yes,' came the reply. 'I've just finished registering.'

'And you've watched the film in its entirety?'

'Yes, twice.'

'That's not nearly enough.'

'But I don't need to see it anymore.'

'Yes, you do.'

'Why?'

'Because you're failing to display sufficient enthusiasm.'

'But I am enthusiastic!'

'Prove it then.'

'Well, how many times do I have to see it?'

'As many as it takes.'

With that he was turned around and led back inside the stadium. We could still hear his protests as he disappeared into the gloom. Meanwhile the film about Lee Montana was starting once again.

'Come on,' said Rupert. 'Let's go.'

We walked swiftly back to the car and got in.

'Most extraordinary,' I said. 'I thought the whole idea of registration was to dispel the chaos: to filter the hordes of confirmed witnesses into a manageable flow. Clearly it's gone far beyond that now. The park authority has become a law unto itself.'

'Very well put,' said Rupert, 'and furthermore I suspect there's a guiding hand behind it all.'

'You mean the president?'

'No, his son-in-law.'

'Ah, yes.'

We drove hurriedly back the way we'd come. Neither of us was in a very talkative mood so there was little conversation. After about two miles I noticed someone walking along the side of the road. I took my foot off the pedal and slowed down to offer them a ride.

'Don't stop,' said Rupert. 'It's Hartley.'

'Oh, yes,' I said. 'So it is.'

Because the road was empty I'd been driving with the headlights on main beam. When he heard the car approaching Hartley looked around and raised his hand to shield his eyes from the glare. I killed the lights momentarily before speeding past him; then I switched them on again. In the mirror I could see Hartley peering after the car in bewilderment. He was quickly lost from view.

'Do you think he recognised us?' I asked.

'Not sure,' said Rupert. 'Depends how good his eyesight is.'

'I feel a bit bad about leaving him behind.'

'He'll be home soon enough.'

When we got back to the gatehouse we took great care to position the black sedan exactly where it had been prior to our departure. Rupert said goodnight and made his way into the darkness. I closed the gate and went inside, hanging the car keys on the rack before giving the place a general tidy up. After about half an hour I put the kettle on. I was just pouring the tea when the door opened and Hartley came in. He'd been gone for a day and a half but I pretended it was only about ten minutes.

'Aha,' I said. 'You're back already.'

I fussed around with a cup and saucer and sat him down at the table, never allowing him a chance to question what I'd been doing while he was away. It struck me that he wore a rather glazed expression. Once or twice I thought I saw him glancing at the key rack but if he had any suspicions he didn't voice them. Plainly there were more important matters on his mind.

'Get registered okay?' I enquired.

'Indeed, yes,' he replied. 'Marvellous experience.'

From his inside pocket he produced a number of items which he laid carefully on the table. They included his official certificate of registration and pristine copies of the leaflets that had fallen from the sky; also a slim pamphlet, some postcards and a few bookmarks.

'This should encourage you,' he said, offering the pamphlet to me.

I saw immediately that the cover illustration was based on the original grainy image of a girl on an elephant. Expert hands had enhanced the picture so that it now had a kind of glossy sheen which wasn't to my taste at all. Nevertheless I gave an approving nod and started turning the pages. Inside were further illustrations depicting a fanciful 'journey' during which she progressed through an idyllic landscape of fields, rivers and wooded escarpments. (I presumed this was meant to represent the British Isles rather than the African savannah.) An accompanying text explained that the search for the girl on the elephant was a righteous cause. I was aware that Hartley was watching me closely so I made a point of studying each picture for several seconds before moving to the next. On the last page was an exhortation to get registered. I smiled and nodded again and handed the pamphlet back.

'No, keep it, please,' he insisted. 'I got it especially for you.'

'Oh, right, thanks.'

'You can go along and register tomorrow if you wish. I'll look after the gate in your absence.'

Over the remainder of the evening Hartley reiterated several times that he'd undergone a marvellous experience and after a while I began to wonder whether he was trying to convince me or himself. He didn't specifically mention the ten minute film but I guessed he must have been subjected to countless repeat viewings during his sojourn at the Eastbrook Stadium. Evidently the desired effect had been achieved. He was now a fully-confirmed witness.

Needless to say I had no intention of registering. I retired to my bunk wondering how I could extricate myself from the situation. Fortunately Rupert provided a perfect solution. Around two o'clock I was woken by a tremendous crash a short distance away. Instantly I got up and went to the kitchen to put my boots on. Moments later a bleary-eyed Hartley appeared in the bedroom doorway.

'Did you hear that?' he asked.

'Yes,' I said, 'but it's my turn to go and investigate. You can go back to bed if you like.'

'Are you sure?'

'Of course.'

'Well, I must admit I haven't had much sleep lately.'

'There you are then.'

He lent me his torch and I headed into the night.

Rupert had chosen his target well. I didn't have to walk very far before I found a neatly felled telegraph pole lying clear of the main road and causing no blockage. The grass nearby was trampled flat.

'Are you quite alone?' said a voice in the darkness.

'Yes,' I answered.

Rupert emerged from the shadows and by the light of the torch we surveyed his workmanship.

'Most satisfactory,' he said. 'A feather in Hartley's cap without any of the usual inconvenience.'

'Yes,' I agreed. 'He'll be delighted.'

Rupert departed and I trudged back to the gatehouse. The following morning I got up early and put on my uniform before joining Hartley in the kitchen for breakfast. I told him about the fallen pole and how it could definitely be ascribed to the girl on the elephant. He was indeed delighted at the news.

'Were you able to catch a glimpse of her?' he asked.

'I'm afraid not,' I replied. 'Too dark.'

'Never mind,' he said. 'It still counts.'

'I'll go and register this morning.'

Hartley advised me that things were so busy at the Eastbrook Stadium that it might be a couple of days before I was properly registered. He was certain he could manage the gate on his own until I returned. Meanwhile I should make the most of a marvellous experience.

'Just come back when you're ready,' he said.

'Alright. Thanks.'

My plan was to set off on foot towards the stadium and then double back via a side road and make for Rupert's hideout. We would then decide on our next move. Before I could get going, however, a horn hooted and a park authority van pulled up outside the gatehouse.

'That's a bit of luck,' said Hartley. 'They can give you a lift.'

'Oh, well, I was thinking of walking.'

'No, no, if you go with them you'll be there in a jiffy. I'm sure they'll have plenty of room in the van.'

He led me outside to meet the driver. It was the same guy who'd been so disdainful of me on our previous encounter: the one who'd called me a doubting Thomas. He was reluctant to take me aboard but Hartley persevered and eventually I was allowed to squeeze in the back with the others. They were equally unwelcoming. As we passed through the gate I prepared myself for a less than pleasant trip. It was supposed to be four miles but after only a minute the van stopped again. There was a brief delay as everybody piled out to examine the recently-felled telegraph pole.

Notes were taken and the damage was recorded in the log book before we resumed the journey. I felt very much out of place. Occasionally one of the men would scrutinise my park authority uniform (which was now beginning to lose some of its crispness) but by and large they ignored me. Plainly I was deemed to be unworthy of their company.

I soon learned that the van's destination wasn't the Eastbrook Stadium itself. Apparently Hartley had got his facts wrong. The men were actually heading for the interior and would be dropping me off at a junction about a mile away from the stadium. This suited me fine although it put paid to any idea of doubling back to Rupert's place. In the past few minutes we'd skirted several roundabouts and when they finally deposited me at the kerbside I had no real idea where I was. My only reference point was a sign directing me to the stadium (distance: one mile) but as I said before I had no intention of going there. As soon as I got out of the van the door was slammed shut from inside and it drove off. Once again I was all alone.

9

Some distance away I could see an object glinting in the sunshine. A number of large playing fields lay to one side of the road and from the furthest corner there came an occasional flash of light. It was obvious that no games or sports had been played here for a good few years so I wondered what the source could be. Unaccountably the distant glimmer of light stirred inside me a profound sense of hopefulness. In fact I felt myself being drawn towards it by an irresistible force. The feeling was redolent of a long-forgotten episode that I couldn't quite put my finger on: a happy memory with all the details lost. I gazed over the enormous expanse of playing fields. The grass was long and unkempt but I noticed it had been flattened in places. On closer inspection I discovered a trail of wheel marks where a vehicle had recently crossed it. The trail led all the way to the corner of the furthest field. I followed it and as I drew nearer the object gradually took shape. I thought it looked vaguely familiar and then suddenly I recognised the glasshouse on wheels. It was parked on a concrete apron (possibly the site of a former clubhouse) and somebody was moving around it polishing the glass. For a few seconds I paused to watch. I was still about thirty yards away but now I had a clear view of the person applying the polish.

It was Ambrose.

He was very busy with his task and hadn't seen me coming. I continued strolling towards him. The vehicle had many windows and they were all sparkling clean but it seemed he hadn't finished yet. He took a fresh cloth from a box and began going round again giving them a final 'dry' polish. For a while he was lost from view as he attended to the far side; then eventually he reappeared and saw me standing there.

'Oh, hello,' he said. 'How did you get on at the independent settlement?'

'It was rather disappointing,' I replied. 'I was forcibly ejected.'

Whenever I encountered Ambrose I always experienced a mixture of elation and guilt. Today was no exception. He was the type of person who always considered others before himself. He'd come to my aid on several occasions in the past but I'd never made any effort to pay him back. I thought of his black sedan stuck in a compound less than five miles away and pondered whether I should mention it to him. Considering how much I owed him it was really the least I could do. When I remembered the confiscated lunchboxes, however, I realised I could face some awkward questions. Ultimately, therefore, I decided on a more circuitous approach.

'I see you've got yourself a new set of wheels,' I observed.

'Yes,' he said. 'It's a research vehicle. Would you like to have a look around?'

'Okay, if you can spare the time.'

'Of course.'

He then took me on a short guided tour. The four-wheeled vehicle had a low chassis about twenty feet long and eight feet wide with lights fitted front and rear. The driver's seat was situated on the left and sticking up through the bare metal floor were the foot pedals, the steering column, the handbrake and the gear lever. There was a basic instrument panel comprising a speedometer and an oil pressure gauge. Rising above the chassis was an oblong metal framework about nine feet high. This supported numerous glass panels that formed the upper body of the vehicle. (It was these glass panels that I'd seen glinting in the distance.) The engine was mounted behind a bulkhead at the very back.

There were no passenger seats and the only items on board were a clothes trunk and a large hamper.

'Had any lunch?' Ambrose enquired.

'No,' I said, 'I haven't.'

He went to the hamper and produced a lunch box.

'Quite warm in here, isn't it?' he remarked. 'Let's go outside.'

After we'd shared lunch he completed his polishing; he then opened a metal flap to give the engine a thorough examination. It struck me as unlikely that Ambrose had come to the furthest corner of this field merely to have a picnic but for the moment I couldn't think of any alternative explanation. He had his usual purposeful look about him and I could only assume there must be some overarching motive behind his actions. When I asked if there was anything I could do to help he politely declined the offer. Instead I just stood around and tried not to get in his way. The research vehicle was now looking very spick-and-span as it gleamed in the sunshine.

A little later we heard a horn hooting over on the main road. A convoy of cars pulled up at the edge of the playing fields and a few people got out and gathered into a group. They were evidently discussing some important matter. One or two of them pointed in our direction and then the leading car turned off the road and began driving across the field towards us.

'Here they come,' murmured Ambrose. 'Yet more victims of delusion.'

The car was upon us in no time. The occupants were two men and two women, all fairly young and all wearing T-shirts emblazoned with the letters: CW

'Don't bother wasting your time here,' said one of the men. 'There's been a sighting about ten miles away by the railway viaduct.'

He addressed his words to me, presumably because I was wearing a park authority uniform.

'Oh, right,' I said. 'Thanks for letting us know.'

'Actually we're here on other business,' added Ambrose.

He might as well have been speaking a foreign language. The man regarded him with a serene expression for several seconds.

'No, no, not here,' he said at length. 'About ten miles away. By the railway viaduct.'

All four of them were smiling condescendingly at Ambrose and me as though we were small children who'd failed to comprehend the delights that awaited us. Over at the roadside one of the waiting cars honked its horn impatiently. They were all plainly raring to go.

'We're on our way there now,' said the man. 'You can follow behind if you wish.'

'Okay,' I replied. 'Thanks.'

They all smiled and waved as the car sped away across the playing fields and rejoined the convoy. Soon they were all on the move, heading west. There was a further honking of horns and then they were lost from view.

Ambrose shook his head before turning to me.

'You're aware, of course, that there's no girl and no elephant?'

I knew for a fact that his assertion wasn't entirely accurate: I'd seen both girl and elephant with my own eyes in another part of the British Isles. Nonetheless I understood the gist of what he was saying.

'Maybe so,' I ventured, 'but the belief is widespread.'

'It's turning into a national movement.'

'Unstoppable.'

'Well, we'll see about that.'

For a few moments he peered over the playing fields and into the distance beyond, then abruptly he began stalking towards the research vehicle. I noticed he had a sudden spring in his step.

'Come on,' he said, over his shoulder. 'Let's follow them and investigate.'

Soon he was in the driving seat. He instructed me to sit on the clothes trunk and then he pressed a switch. As the engine roared into life all the glass panels started to rattle in their frames. He selected a gear and heaved on the wheel, raising his voice above the noise.

'I'm afraid there's no power steering!'

The research vehicle trundled across the grass and onto the main road. Ambrose proceeded with care, gradually gathering momentum until we reached 20mph. He raised his voice again.

'That's our maximum speed!' he announced. 'Any faster and the glass will break!'

I gazed at the playing fields receding slowly behind us and wondered how we could possibly catch up with the convoy that had sped away so swiftly. Ambrose appeared unconcerned, however, and I guessed he knew the location of the railway viaduct they'd mentioned. The clothes trunk wasn't particularly uncomfortable so I tried to enjoy the ride as best I could.

The surrounding landscape was changing again. There were derelict buildings on either side of the road with trees and bushes growing through them; the verges were thick with vegetation and mosses thrived on the walls and rooftops. It seemed that the long spell of mild weather had done its work effectively. The swathes of greenery were forever on the march and I realised there were many places which could feasibly provide fodder for a roving menagerie. Even so there was no question that all those confirmed witnesses were destined for disappointment. Ambrose evidently held similar (but not identical) views to me and I was interested to see where his 'investigation' would lead.

We weren't the only vehicle on the road. Our sluggish pace meant that we were constantly being overtaken by convoys of cars and vans all going in the same direction as us. Clearly word had got around about the latest sighting. We also passed groups and individuals travelling on foot. To my profound relief Ambrose didn't stop to pick up any pedestrians. Nor did he offer assistance to motorists who'd broken down. It was in his nature to help other people but I suspected he was becoming a little wary of the confirmed witnesses and wanted to keep them at arm's length.

Plainly a few of them thought that we ourselves were on the verge of breaking down. On several occasions we received curious looks from the occupants of overtaking cars as if they were unable to understand why we were travelling so slowly. I had to admit that I probably wouldn't have had the patience to dawdle along for mile upon mile but to his credit Ambrose continued undaunted.

After about half an hour a railway embankment appeared behind a long row of terraced houses on our right-hand side. For a while we ran parallel to the line as it crossed a series of bridges before vanishing into some woodland. The road descended in a curve around the woods and when we reached the far side we saw a huge viaduct spanning a valley. The railway was now high above us supported by immense red brick arches. Down to our left was a broad stream running through abandoned farmland. After we'd passed under the viaduct the valley opened up again to reveal countless fields and hedges. In the distance some chimneys and cooling towers signalled that we were heading towards yet another conurbation. Ambrose stopped at the roadside.

'Look at that,' he said.

Just beyond the nearest hedge a large flag was fluttering in the breeze. It had a green background and depicted a grey elephant with white tusks. The elephant was walking with one foot raised slightly above the ground.

'Very professional,' remarked Ambrose knowledgeably. 'Elephant passant, I believe.'

Further along the road was an open gate where three or four people stood beckoning us to enter. Ambrose pulled forward and as we drew closer I saw they were all wearing T-shirts emblazoned with the letters: CW

'Are we going in?' I enquired.

'Well, I'll have to take it easy,' said Ambrose. 'The gateway's a bit narrow and this vehicle's got a restricted turning circle.'

As a matter of fact I hadn't been referring to the practical difficulties of entering the field: I was more concerned with the wisdom of getting too closely involved with all these zealots.

Through the hedge we could now see scores of cars and vans alongside brightly-coloured tents and yet more flags. Presumably they were holding some kind of rally here to celebrate the confirmed sighting. Judging by the numbers it was a popular event and the idea of joining in made me feel uneasy. Up until this moment I'd taken it for granted that we would conduct a low-profile investigation: I'd envisaged us as detached observers slightly removed from the masses. Now, though, it seemed Ambrose was considering driving into their midst.

'Why don't we park half a mile up the road and walk back to have a look?' I suggested.

'Oh, we can't do that,' he replied. 'It's a research vehicle. We must never leave it unattended.'

He indicated to the people at the gate that he needed a little space. They stood back and he then began manoeuvring in a wide arc, taking up the whole road as he did so. There were now a couple of other cars waiting behind us. I was expecting any second to hear a volley of irritable honks on horns but actually they were all quite patient. There was virtually a holiday atmosphere about the place and when Ambrose successfully negotiated the gateway he was rewarded with a friendly round of applause. A few helpful people emerged from their tents to direct us to a suitable space. Others simply gathered around to admire the sparkling glass. I took a deep breath. We were now surrounded on all sides by the confirmed witnesses we were supposed to be keeping at arm's length. Despite his earlier caution Ambrose had made a very audacious move. I only hoped his judgment was correct.

10

Once we were settled in I left Ambrose giving the research vehicle another polish and went to have a look around. The field was quite large and extended all the way down to the foot of the viaduct where a wooden bridge crossed a stream. It was the perfect setting for a rally: the grass was lush and the enormous red brick arches formed an attractive backdrop to the accompanying hustle and bustle. Alongside the tents, cars and vans I discovered that many people had set up stalls selling all manner of items. Needless to say the ubiquitous CONFIRMED WITNESS T-shirts were widely available, as well as postcards, bumper stickers and pennants, all bearing the image of the elephant 'passant'. There was also a range of souvenir coins incorporating the same design. At least I assumed they were souvenir coins because they were too shiny to be real. As I continued to wander amongst the stalls, however, I saw them changing hands with each purchase as if they were normal currency. I soon learned that they weren't actually coins at all: they were tokens. Personally I hadn't seen any proper money since I left the western gate several months earlier. In consequence I was a bit out of touch. I certainly had no inkling that an alternative currency had gone into circulation. Nevertheless it struck me as odd that these tokens bore the same image as the goods on sale. Everywhere I looked I saw the elephant 'passant' reproduced in some form or other, most prominently in the flags that fluttered overhead, to the total exclusion of all other symbols. It seemed that the confirmed witnesses saw the world through a very narrow spectrum.

What they all had in common, of course, was their ardent conviction that a sighting had taken place near the viaduct. Yet when I asked for more details I received only vague answers. None of the stallholders were able to tell me the exact location of the sighting and when I persisted they became increasingly evasive. Some of them glared at me accusingly as though I had no right to be casting doubts. Others peered warily at my park authority uniform: perhaps they thought they'd be in trouble if they gave the wrong reply. Either way the unerring firmness of their belief was rather alarming to observe. Henceforward I ceased asking questions.

When finally I returned to the research vehicle I found Ambrose sorting through the clothes trunk. Apparently it contained not only clothes but bedding as well. He issued me with some blankets, sheets and a pillow.

'I'm afraid you'll have to sleep on the floor,' he said. 'That's what I've been doing for a few weeks now and I've got quite used to it.'

Needless to say there were no curtains in the glasshouse on wheels. We were in full view of our immediate neighbours and could expect no privacy. Fortunately for us they were all planning an early night in anticipation of a hue and cry the following day. No sooner had darkness fallen than the stallholders closed their shutters, then everyone began to disperse. Soon they were all in bed. Ambrose and I shared a lunchbox and I told him what I'd seen while I was moseying around. When I mentioned the tokens he surprised me by producing a few from his pocket.

'They were amongst the small change last time I bought some fuel,' he explained. 'I didn't notice until later.'

'Where was that then?'

'Over by the coast. You can't get fuel anywhere inland.'

'No, I suppose not.'

He reflected for a few moments.

'That reminds me,' he said, 'A few weeks ago I loaned my black sedan to those three sunbathers. Lenny, Zoony and Terry their names were. Do you remember them?'

'Er...yes,' I said. 'Just about.'

'They were doing me a favour actually. I'd just picked up this research vehicle and I asked them to take temporary charge of the black sedan. I said they could borrow it for a month or so. The only trouble was that it urgently needed refuelling. I hope they made it to the coast okay.'

'They probably did.'

In the light of recent events I thought it best to change the subject.

'The hue and cry,' I said, 'appears to be the preferred modus operandi of the park authority.'

'Yes,' replied Ambrose, 'so I understand.'

'A mistaken approach if you ask me.'

Indeed I was astounded that the confirmed witnesses were prepared to participate in such heavy-handed practices. Hitherto I'd been under the impression that their movement was dedicated to safeguarding the girl on the elephant; in which case surely the answer would be simply to leave her in peace. A well-orchestrated hue and cry, on the other hand, could only serve to drive her into the open. Oh yes, they'd be certain to get their confirmed sighting. Ultimately, however, the cause would be lost.

Clearly the men who ran the park authority were immune to these misgivings. Their sole intention was to round up the elephant, the zebras, the ostriches and the young giraffe and return them to their own country (wherever that happened to be). Meanwhile they peddled the notion that Great Britain would somehow be transformed into a sanctuary. They got people to register for the campaign in their thousands; they sent them out on fruitless searches and encouraged them with icons, flags and trinkets. Naturally the British public fell for it all.

I pondered these matters as I laid out my bedding and prepared for my first night under glass. Ambrose had placed the clothes trunk between us so that we both occupied our own separate 'rooms'. Even so I suspected I wouldn't get much sleep. Silence had descended over the field but every time there was a slight gust of wind the entire structure creaked and rattled. Why Ambrose required a vehicle made largely from glass was beyond me. It was cumbersome, slow and entirely unsuited to the disintegrating roads. Nonetheless he'd temporarily exchanged it for his black sedan so presumably he considered it useful. Accordingly I made a mental note to ask him the exact purpose of the research he was conducting.

As I lay gazing into the darkness I half-expected any minute to hear a distant crash. I wouldn't have put it past the park authority to stage the felling of a convenient telegraph pole in order to further justify the rally. Rupert had become quite adept at engineering such demonstrations so I knew how readily it could be done. In the event, though, we had a relatively peaceful night. Far from keeping me awake the creaks and rattles actually lulled me to sleep and the next thing I knew there was daylight beaming in. Outside I could see people beginning to roam around so I swiftly rose and dressed. Ambrose was already up and about.

'They're all heading in the same direction,' he said. 'I think we'd better skip breakfast and go after them.'

I didn't really like the idea of 'skipping breakfast' (in my view it was the most important meal of the day) but as I was Ambrose's guest I really had no choice. We soon discovered that everybody was hastening towards the wooden bridge that spanned the stream beneath the viaduct. Beyond the bridge was a second field where a number of park authority officials were issuing instructions. I had no idea where they'd materialised from: I was sure they hadn't been around when we first arrived and I guessed they must have been bussed in especially for the occasion. They were ordering people to fan out across adjacent fields. I tried to avoid going too near them in case they noticed my uniform but actually they were so busy that I was able to pass unseen. Most of those involved in the hue and cry were chattering with excitement and I could hear cow bells clanging along the lines as they slowly moved forward from one field to the next. Some were carrying banners depicting the elephant 'passant'. Others beat on drums. I had to admit that as a feat of organisation it was most impressive. Whenever a narrow gateway threatened to cause congestion there were additional officials on hand to give directions and maintain discipline. The shape of the line would then be swiftly restored and move forward once again.

Eventually a large hilly field opened out before us. The broad stream meandered along its furthermost boundary and beyond it lay thick woodland that was plainly impenetrable. Somebody called a halt as a murmur of disappointment spread along the ranks. The way ahead was effectively blocked.

There was a brief delay in proceedings and people began milling around in an aimless manner. Down by the stream a group of officials stood in conference together. They seemed to be studying a stretch of mud and I assumed they were searching for hoof prints. The seething throng stirred expectantly. One of the officials was standing slightly aloof from the others. All of a sudden he gave a cry of triumph before turning towards the waiting multitude and holding a pair of imaginary binoculars to his eyes. This, apparently, was the signal that a sighting had been confirmed: the girl on the elephant had indeed passed close by. There followed a round of jubilant cheering, handshakes and general self-congratulation. When a few individuals attempted to approach the stream for a closer look, however, they were waved away by the officials. Within minutes everyone was being herded back towards the viaduct, all buzzing with delight at their good fortune. It struck me that I'd just witnessed crowd control par excellence.

Yet there was still more to come. Another man in a park authority uniform hurried down from the encampment and spoke urgently to his colleagues by the stream. Soon they were all rushing back to the main road where a large van awaited them. Before they departed they passed word around that another sighting had been made near the woollen mill about fifteen miles away. The news was enough to trigger a spontaneous exodus from the field. People began swiftly packing away tents and loading their cars. They were on the move again.

I returned to the research vehicle and waited for Ambrose to reappear. We'd become separated during the hue and cry but I knew he couldn't be far away. As it transpired, though, it took him quite a while to come back. Finally I spotted him trudging up from the viaduct. I wandered down to meet him.

'I took a circular route,' he explained. 'I wanted to have a discreet look at that stretch of mud.'

'Don't tell me,' I said. 'No hoof prints.'

'On the contrary. There were lots of them.'

'Good grief.'

'Whether they were authentic, of course, is a different question altogether.'

I told him about the new sighting near the woollen mill.

'Well,' he said, 'I think we'd better skip lunch and go after them.'

I absorbed his words with dismay. Not only had he decided to skip breakfast but now it was lunch as well! As I folded away my bedding and put it in the clothes trunk, I realised I was now fully dependent on Ambrose. It followed that for the time being I was obliged to abide by his every whim and fancy. If he chose to skip meals then I had no option other than to comply. As a matter of fact it would have been unfair to describe his way of life as 'whimsical': from what I'd seen he endured a spartan existence with no thought for his own comfort. Furthermore he had a generous streak which rendered him almost virtuous. If he had any faults I was yet to encounter them.

Just before we set off I had a final glance around the field and noticed that not quite everybody had decided to leave. Down by the wooden bridge a circle of cars and tents had been established. People were at work sawing timber and digging the foundations for some kind of building. On a pole above them fluttered a flag depicting the elephant 'passant'.

'Seems as if a few of them have decided to settle here,' I remarked. 'They must have found whatever they've been searching for.'

After a few moments of quiet contemplation Ambrose went to the hamper and removed half a dozen lunchboxes.

'They're going to face difficulties in their early days,' he said, 'especially when autumn approaches. I think we'll make a goodwill gesture.'

With that he picked up the lunchboxes and carried them across the field towards the nascent settlement. When he was at a safe distance I raised the lid of the hamper and counted the remaining lunchboxes. There were seven in total. Even the sight of them made me feel hungry so I quickly closed the lid again and busied myself polishing the glass. I had a feeling the next few hours would be a struggle but I was determined to go through with it. I reasoned that if Ambrose could go without breakfast and lunch then so could I.

When he returned he made no mention of the settlers but merely climbed into the driving seat and started the engine. A minute later we were inching carefully through the gateway and out onto the road. We slowly gathered speed until we reached 20mph. The idea of pursuing a convoy that had departed almost half an hour ahead of us suddenly appeared preposterous. Most of the cars had sped off at full pelt and were probably miles away before we even started. Still, there was no alternative except to plod steadily along in their wake. Ambrose gave no indication whether he knew the location of the woollen mill but by now I had developed an unreserved faith in his capabilities.

As we rumbled along that road, however, I became aware of a vague feeling of irritation. It was hardly anything at first, barely discernible, but it was there alright and during the course of the journey it nagged at me more and more. The incessant rattling and creaking that had lulled me to sleep in the night began gradually to get on my nerves. Ambrose was having to circumnavigate some serious ruts and potholes and every slight jolt went right through me. To make matters worse the sunlight was blazing mercilessly through the panes of glass. In consequence I soon developed a headache. I tried closing my eyes but that didn't help. The tedium was unrelenting and in due course the irritation gave way to lethargy. I lost interest in the journey and gazed listlessly at the passing landscape.

We had now left the countryside and once again there were dilapidated buildings all around us. The derelict cooling towers and chimneys suggested we were entering a region that had been depressed even before the time of the purchase. No wonder the inhabitants had abandoned the place and migrated to the coast!

There was very little in the way of open space and I found it difficult to believe that the roving menagerie would have headed in this direction. Yet Ambrose just kept on going so I assumed we were still on the right track.

His perseverance astounded me. To my knowledge he'd gone without food for at least eighteen hours but still he showed no sign of flagging. He drove like a professional: both hands on the wheel and paying constant attention to his mirrors and speedometer. 20mph was the limit and he made sure he kept to it. Meanwhile my personal suffering increased exponentially.

At some point I heard myself stifling a yawn. I must have made more noise than I intended because Ambrose glanced at me over his shoulder.

'You alright?' he asked.

'Yes,' I replied. 'Fine thanks.'

'Well done,' he said. 'You're doing very well.'

Far from being comforted by this remark I was overcome with profound disgruntlement. All at once it became obvious that the enforced period of fasting was some sort of test administered by Ambrose to measure my resolve. Well two could play at that game! From then on I sat bolt upright on the clothes trunk with my arms folded and watched his every move as though I was examining his driving. In this manner we pressed on for many miles. The research vehicle trundled into the heart of an immense former industrial district now bathed in unseasonal sunshine.

At long last we saw ahead of us the sign of the elephant 'passant'. Someone had draped a banner across the front of an immense brick building and there were cars and vans parked all around it. To my surprise, though, Ambrose drove straight past without stopping.

'Wasn't that the woollen mill?' I enquired.

'Correct,' said Ambrose, 'but this vehicle is rather conspicuous. If we keep turning up at their events they might suspect we're following them.'

'Well, we are.'

He gave a nod of acknowledgment.

'Nevertheless, I think we'll park out of sight on this occasion.'

We drove for another quarter of a mile and then turned into a side road. Ambrose reversed into a yard between some lock-up garages and switched the engine off. He then announced that he would go and investigate while I took care of the vehicle.

'On no account leave it unattended,' he enjoined before walking briskly back along the road.

I was glad he hadn't asked me to go with him. I wasn't in the mood for investigating anything and, besides, I still had a headache. Instead I lolled in the driving seat staring languidly through the windscreen. Unfortunately I soon discovered that doing nothing was just as bad. There was only a series of green-painted garage doors to look at and I swiftly became bored. My head was pounding so eventually I went out to get some fresh air. I wandered around the yard casually trying some of the locks before straying onto the side road where I'd last seen Ambrose. A full half hour had gone by since he'd departed and there was still no sign of him returning. The research vehicle seemed quite safe to me so I strolled down to the main road and peered around the corner in the direction of the woollen mill. I couldn't fathom why Ambrose was taking such a long time to come back and I was beginning to feel slightly worried. Maybe the lack of sustenance affected my judgement because I then decided to go in search of him. I reckoned that if I spotted him in the distance I could easily get back to the yard first and he would never know I'd deserted my post.

I approached the woollen mill with caution while keeping a sharp eye on the entrance. A number of people were going in and out and when I got nearer I noticed they were all wearing T-shirts proclaiming their status as confirmed witnesses. Likewise, most of the cars and vans parked outside had enamel CW plates or bumper stickers. After some hesitation I entered the building and saw that the machinery for milling wool had long since been removed. Now the entire space was given over to rows and rows of trestle tables laden with all kinds of memorabilia: pennants, engravings, pictures and statuettes. There were banners suspended beneath the ceiling and the walls were adorned with life size images of the elephant 'passant'. I recognised some of the stallholders from the previous rally and drew the obvious conclusion: the ecological campaign had evolved into a commercial racket!

All those so-called 'confirmed sightings' were merely ploys to attract customers to a rundown industrial district that couldn't possibly support the roving menagerie. I watched in disbelief as hundreds of enthusiasts swirled around the trestle tables purchasing yet more souvenirs and paying for them with tokens which they'd presumably exchanged for hard-earned cash. As I stood in the midst of all this I felt my head beginning to spin. All I could hear was the babbling of excited voices augmented by the shuffling of feet. I hadn't eaten a morsel all day long and it was beginning to tell. A nearby stall was selling cakes and buns but when I made enquiries I was informed that they only accepted the new tokens. I realised I'd made a big mistake coming here. The atmosphere was noisy and oppressive and I desperately needed to get out. I was just heading for the exit when I heard a voice raised in anger.

'There is no girl,' it declared, 'and there is no elephant!'

These were the exact words that Ambrose had uttered a day or two earlier. I knew it couldn't be him making such a fuss yet the voice was slightly familiar. Within seconds a kerfuffle broke out a few yards away from me. The crowd parted momentarily and I was astonished to see who was at the centre of the disturbance. It was Brock: my captor from the stadium in the midland counties. He stood raving at the people all around him, loudly repeating his contention that there was no girl and no elephant. Understandably he was met with hostility. Some bystanders jeered at him. Others laughed. In a fit of rage he began overturning the tables and spilling merchandise everywhere.

'There is no girl,' he roared, 'and there is no elephant!'

Personally I wasn't very keen on Brock. He lacked all social graces and was far too authoritarian for my liking. Even so I feared for his safety. He was surrounded by fanatical zealots who began jostling him roughly towards the exit. I glanced all about me and saw that I was the only person in uniform. Quickly I moved forward and placed myself between Brock and his antagonists.

'Alright!' I said. 'That'll do!'

'But he's a doubting Thomas!' protested one of them. 'We should drive him out.'

'Stand aside!'

The sight of my uniform was enough to make the mob back off. With extreme difficulty I managed to hustle Brock through the exit and outside. He then stalked away offering no word of thanks.

'Don't expect any more help from me,' I murmured. 'You're on your own now.'

I was in a foul temper with the world, with Brock, with the confirmed witnesses and with myself. I could hardly think straight but I knew I urgently needed to get to the lock-up garages before Ambrose returned. I hurried along as quickly as I could but when I reached the yard I saw that he'd beaten me to it. He was hard at work polishing the glass panes and paid no attention to me.

'Sorry about that,' I said, 'but I got worried when you didn't come back.'

Ambrose ignored me and continued with his polishing. I stood watching awkwardly as he progressed along the far side of the research vehicle. Briefly I lost sight of him but then suddenly I heard the engine starting. There was a short delay before he appeared in the doorway.

'Are you coming then?' he demanded.

'Yes, of course.'

I dashed forward and jumped inside. Ambrose was already in the driving seat and we were soon heading across the yard. I was uncertain whether or not he'd forgiven me for my negligence so I merely sat on the clothes trunk and said nothing more. Half a minute later we turned onto the main road.

11

We hadn't gone very far when we saw Brock sitting on the kerb with his head in his hands.

'Hello,' said Ambrose. 'Who's this poor fellow?'

I was tempted to inform him that the 'poor fellow' was called Brock; that he was a former high-ranking figure in the park authority; and that he was now a renegade. I sensed, however, that whatever I said would make no difference. Therefore I remained silent as Ambrose pulled over and stopped. Brock looked up and peered with bewilderment at the glasshouse on wheels. He rose slowly to his feet and Ambrose spoke to him through the window.

'Have you eaten recently?'

'No,' said Brock.

'Come on board then.'

Ambrose got out of the driving seat and went to the hamper. He raised the lid and removed a lunchbox which he passed to Brock. Only as an apparent afterthought did he take out two more: one for himself and one (thankfully) for me. He made it clear that there was no question of our guzzling the contents immediately. Instead we drove on for another mile or so until he spotted a suitable lay-by where he halted and switched off the engine. During the short journey Brock sat beside me on the clothes trunk. He gave no indication of ever having seen me before and I didn't bother introducing myself. When Ambrose finally signalled that we could commence eating I tried to open my lunchbox in a dignified manner but for some reason I couldn't get the lid off. This was rather embarrassing because I'd opened several in the past without any problem. Today, though, because I was so hungry I was all fingers and

183

thumbs. After I'd been fumbling with the lunchbox for several seconds Brock reached over and took it from me. He then handed it back without the lid.

I had no idea what conclusions Ambrose had reached following his visit to the woollen mill. He didn't say if he'd completed his investigation and I didn't ask. In the meantime we'd acquired an additional passenger. When eventually we got going again Brock went and leaned on the bulkhead at the rear of the research vehicle. He looked very subdued and was a markedly changed person from the uniformed martinet who'd presided over my internment. Now he had the haunted demeanour of someone whose empire had collapsed around him: his fall from favour within the park authority had turned him into an outcast who plainly needed to be handled with care. Evidently he held similar views to Ambrose about the girl on the elephant (though his views were more violently expressed). I knew for certain that they were both wrong but for the moment I kept the truth to myself.

After we'd been travelling for a few miles I happened to glance back at Brock. He was gazing intently through the rear window. Something had caught his attention but from my position on the clothes trunk I couldn't see what it was. We trundled on at a stately 20mph and in due course he came to the front and spoke to Ambrose.

'I suppose you're aware we're being followed?'

'Yes,' said Ambrose. 'I can see them in my mirror.'

I went to the rear window and looked out. Behind us was a long convoy of cars and vans. They were making no effort to overtake even on stretches of road where it was perfectly safe to do so. Instead they stuck on our tail as if we were purposely leading them somewhere. Ambrose studied them in his mirror.

'I thought this might happen,' he remarked. 'They obviously assume we know something that they don't.'

'Why don't you speed up and shake them off?' suggested Brock.

'Oh, I can't do that,' said Ambrose. 'If I go any faster than 20mph the glass will break.'

We carried on like this for another hour. By my estimate there were at least two dozen cars and vans trailing along behind us. As far as I could tell we were heading in a westerly direction but our destination remained obscure. The chimneys, mills and cooling towers had now given way to modern industrial buildings (all derelict). We were unlikely to catch a glimpse of the roving menagerie in this kind of landscape yet the convoy tracked us resolutely for mile after mile. As daylight faded and evening approached

Ambrose began looking out for somewhere suitable to halt for the night.

'We can't simply pull into a lay-by,' he said. 'We ideally need a space for twenty or thirty vehicles.'

'But surely that's not our problem,' I countered. 'We didn't ask them to follow us.'

'On the contrary,' he replied. 'I think it's very much our problem.'

Ambrose's sense of civic responsibility was no doubt highly commendable. Nonetheless the prospect of all these enthusiasts attaching themselves to us was extremely daunting. How would they react, I wondered, when they finally realised their folly?

Ambrose seemed unconcerned. He switched on the headlights and continued into the darkness. With nothing to see except an empty road ahead of us the slowness of the research vehicle became ever more tedious. At every junction we were obliged to pause to examine faded signposts for some clue as to our whereabouts. We had now entered uncharted territory that was unfamiliar even to Ambrose and his failure to carry any maps struck me as completely out of character. Indeed, in terms of research the glasshouse on wheels was very sparsely equipped. There were no dials, gauges, meters or related scientific apparatus: there were only these panes of glass that would shatter if we exceeded 20mph.

Brock had resumed his station at the rear window and he now stood regarding the convoy in silence. I guessed it would suit him better if our pursuers abandoned the chase: he'd come very close to being roughed up by confirmed witnesses at the woollen mill and these people were probably of the same persuasion. On the other hand it was quite possible that he enjoyed confronting his opponents, in which case he was unlikely to be disappointed.

Fairly late in the evening a chain link fence appeared on our left. It ran alongside the road for almost a mile and beyond it was a vast expanse of blackness.

'Looks like a disused aerodrome,' said Ambrose. 'Just the sort of place we're looking for.'

Eventually we came to a gateway beneath an arch constructed from a pair of aircraft wings. Ambrose stopped and I jumped out to see if the gate was locked. It wasn't so I swung it open and Ambrose drove in. He stopped again and gave me some instructions.

'Let them all through and then close the gate behind them,' he said. 'Come and find us when you're ready.'

The research vehicle moved slowly away along a concrete road followed immediately by the convoy of cars and vans. I counted a total of twenty seven and most of them had CW plates or bumper stickers. Many also flew pennants depicting the elephant 'passant'. Their occupants looked harmless enough and seemed reassured by my park authority uniform. Once they'd all passed I closed the gate and walked after them. On either side of the concrete road were swathes of unkempt grass. Ahead of me I could see countless tail lights manoeuvring back and forth and as I drew nearer I saw that a circle of cars and vans was being formed around the research vehicle. It made me smile to think that Ambrose and Brock were now surrounded by confirmed witnesses. For a moment I was tempted to remain outside the circle and observe events as a neutral spectator. In reality, however, I had nowhere to sleep and when I remembered the plentiful supply of bedding (not to mention the lunchboxes) I quickly dismissed the idea. Cautiously I made my way between the cars and vans and rejoined my companions in the research vehicle. Brock was standing guard at the door. He moved aside just enough to let me squeeze past him. I found Ambrose gazing intently through the panes of glass. In the darkness beyond the circle we could hear the sound of metal poles clanking and pegs being hammered into the ground as people erected tents.

'At least they're keeping a respectful distance,' said Ambrose.

'Maybe so,' I replied, 'but we're completely hemmed in. We can't move until they do.'

'Don't worry about that,' he said. 'We'll find a solution in the morning.'

He opened the trunk and began distributing the bedding but then Brock announced that he intended to stay awake all night.

'I'll keep an eye on them,' he said. 'Just in case.'

He could not be persuaded otherwise so we left him to it and got our heads down.

Gradually the external noises faded away until there was only the creaking and rattling of the research vehicle. Once again this lulled me to sleep. At some stage I woke up and saw that Brock was no longer standing in the doorway. I guessed he'd gone out to patrol the area. Soon I drifted off to sleep again. Next time I awoke it was dawn. The creaking and rattling had subsided. I looked outside and instantly spotted Brock. He was working his way along the circle of cars and vans and writing in the dew on their windscreens. I was unable to see what he wrote but I could hazard a guess. Quickly I got up and alerted Ambrose and then the two of us rushed over to the circle. Many windscreens were now inscribed with the words: THERE IS NO GIRL AND THERE IS NO ELEPHANT!

Ambrose quietly remonstrated with Brock.

'We shouldn't antagonise them,' he said. 'There are much better ways to make them understand.'

Somehow he prevailed upon Brock to return to the research vehicle. Meanwhile I took a cloth and went round the cars and vans cleaning off the contentious words. Just as I was finishing the last windscreen a man emerged from a nearby tent.

'What are you doing?' he demanded gruffly.

'Just buffing it up,' I replied with a cheery smile. 'All part of the service.'

He peered at my park authority uniform.

'Oh,' he said, 'are you from the glasshouse on wheels?'

'Yes.'

His tone of voice altered.

'Do you think we'll be offered any guidance today?' he enquired.

'I'm certain you will,' I said. 'In the fullness of time.'

He was seemingly satisfied with my answer. Other people were now beginning to appear from their tents so I wished him good day and cautiously retreated. Ambrose was waiting for me by the research vehicle.

'Come inside,' he said, 'and have some breakfast.'

When he opened the hamper I was surprised to see that it still contained seven lunchboxes. I realised I must have miscounted and thought no more about it. Brock and I were given a box between us which we were obliged to share. I assumed this was because we were both in Ambrose's bad books: me for deserting my post the previous day and Brock for his provocative behaviour. Ambrose didn't say anything but I knew he was cross with the pair of us. After breakfast he got me to help him lift the hamper outside. Once we'd lowered it to the ground I happened to glance towards the circle of cars and vans and noticed that we were under observation. Scores of people were sitting or leaning on their vehicles. They were all scrutinising the glasshouse on wheels and looked as though they were waiting for something to happen.

'How long have they been there?' I asked.

'They started gathering while we were having breakfast,' said Ambrose. 'I suspect they haven't eaten.'

'But surely they must have brought along some supplies.'

'Not necessarily,' he said. 'Don't forget this is an impromptu rally. There were lots of food stalls back at the woollen mill: there are none here.'

With that he raised a hand and beckoned to the onlookers.

'You may approach,' he announced, 'and I will feed you.'

After a brief pause one of them came forward. It was the man who'd caught me cleaning his windscreen at dawn. He approached tentatively until he stood before us. Ambrose then lifted the lid of the hamper and produced a lunchbox which he handed to the man. A second man followed and he also received a lunchbox; then two women; then another man. By my calculation the hamper should now have been empty yet still Ambrose continued calling them to come to him. Soon there were several people approaching at a time and they were each given a lunchbox. Actually some took two or three. Word of Ambrose's generosity was spreading fast and I had a feeling it could swiftly get out of control. Brock was watching proceedings from inside the research vehicle. I signalled him for assistance and together we organised the supplicants into a proper queue. The process lasted quite a while and Ambrose didn't cease work until everyone had been fed. I had no idea how he'd pulled off the trick but in consequence he now had the people at his command. When he spoke they all listened.

'You do not need to seek the girl on the elephant!' he proclaimed. 'She will come and seek you when she is ready!'

Brock was standing nearby and for a moment I thought he was going to voice an objection. He certainly appeared shocked by the assertion: this wasn't the message he'd been imparting in recent days. As Ambrose's words sunk in, however, he must have realised their subtlety. Here was a way out of the impasse by which everybody gained. The confirmed witnesses had received their 'guidance' and were freed from any obligation to pursue the girl on the elephant. We in turn would be released from our encirclement. It was a perfect solution. Some of the people were already beginning to return to their cars and vans in readiness for the journey home. Others were still consuming the contents of their lunchboxes but it clearly wouldn't be long until they followed suit. Brock seemed to understand this and therefore kept his silence. We watched from the confines of the research vehicle as they took down their tents and packed them away. Within an hour the bulk of the convoy had moved out.

'The only trouble is,' said Ambrose, 'there are many more people who are still ignorant of the facts.'

'Yes,' said Brock. 'The park authority has a lot to answer for.'

We all agreed about that.

By now there was only one car remaining. It belonged to the man who'd been first in the queue. He came over to thank Ambrose before he departed.

'If there's anything I can do for you in return,' he said, 'just let me know.'

'Well, actually,' said Ambrose, 'I need to get to the coast. Have you any space in your car?'

'Yes,' came the reply, 'there's plenty of room.'

'Then could I come with you?'

'Of course.'

'I'll join you as well if you don't mind,' said Brock. 'I've got some unfinished business to see to.'

This ad hoc arrangement took me totally by surprise. I asked Ambrose why he simply didn't go to the coast in the research vehicle.

'It's far too slow,' he explained, 'and besides I don't need it any more. My research is complete. I've found out all I need to know.'

'What were you researching then?'

'It was a personal project. I was testing my own patience.'

He delved into a pocket.

'Catch,' he said, tossing me the keys. 'You might as well have it now that it's surplus to requirements.'

The three of them walked back to the car and very soon they were driving across the grass towards the gate.

After they'd gone I raised the lid of the hamper and looked inside. It still contained seven lunchboxes.

12

The confirmed witnesses had left behind a flag bearing the image of the elephant 'passant'. It fluttered high on its pole and was presumably intended to mark the site of the impromptu rally. Given its jolly appearance I thought it was likely to attract unwanted attention so I lowered it and folded it away. For the same reason I decided to move the research vehicle further from the road. After familiarising myself with the controls I started it up and trundled over to the most distant corner of the aerodrome. I switched off the engine and listened to the creaking and rattling as a gentle breeze buffeted the glass panes. It was good to have the whole place to myself after all the turmoil. The sun was shining (though only weakly) and it promised to be another pleasant day.

Beyond the perimeter fence was a wooded valley that led towards some low hills. I walked along the fence in search of a possible way through and after a while I came across a damaged section. I gazed at it in disbelief: it looked as if it had been smashed down by a juggernaut. The ground all about was covered in a variety of hoof prints and as I examined them I felt a surge of euphoria. The trail of prints descended between the trees and into the valley. Without hesitation I followed it as far as a broad stream where it abruptly vanished. I looked all around but found nothing more.

I now had to ask myself whether the trail was genuine. My time with Rupert had taught me that evidence could easily be fabricated. Moreover there were several parties whose interests would be served by yet another 'sighting'. Nevertheless I was convinced my discovery was authentic. The route the trail took from the damaged fence to the stream was noticeably indirect: it wandered this way and that and suggested the unhurried movement of grazing beasts set loose amidst ample foliage. I imagined they had eventually waded into the stream and emerged at some point further along. With diligence it should be possible to find where the trail resumed.

It seemed to me, however, that I'd chosen the wrong time of day for a pursuit that might well prove fruitless. Far better, I reasoned, to return to the valley at dawn next morning and lie in wait until the roving menagerie came to drink. It would require stealth and patience but I was sure this was the best approach.

With my mind made up I went back to the research vehicle and helped myself to a lunchbox. All the time I kept an eye on the main road (I didn't welcome the prospect of being besieged by newly-arrived confirmed witnesses) but thankfully it had gone quiet. I spent a long afternoon enjoying the peace of the glasshouse on wheels; I opened a second lunchbox for supper and around midnight I retired to bed.

For some reason I couldn't sleep. I must have laid there for an hour and a half and still I failed to drift off. By now I was quite accustomed to the creaks and rattles of the research vehicle but after a while I realised there was an additional noise as well. I could hear a slight tapping on the glass like the twigs of a tree swaying nearby. I knew there were no trees on this side of the fence so I pulled the covers over my head and tried to ignore it. The tapping persisted. Eventually I sat up and peered into the gloom. The tapping ceased. There was a little moonlight and gradually I made out the vague figure of a young woman beyond the panes of glass. Then I heard a soft but insistent voice:

'Why don't you leave me alone? All you do is follow me around from one day to the next. You're driving me to distraction.'

'Sorry,' I said. 'I was only trying to help.'

'But you're not helping,' she replied. 'You're only making it worse. Can't you see I don't want you interfering? I've got my own life to live and you're not part of it.'

I could see her glaring at me through the glass. Behind her I discerned an immense brooding presence waiting patiently to carry her away. It made me feel small and insignificant.

'I have to go now,' she said. 'Have I made myself clear?'

'Yes.'

'Good.'

With that she disappeared into the shadows.

13

In the morning I rose early and prepared to leave. I was disappointed at being rejected but not surprised. It had happened to me before and it would probably happen again. Briefly I considered placing a lunchbox beside the stream as a kind of peace offering. Deep down, however, I knew the gesture would achieve nothing. Instead I ate some breakfast before driving slowly across the grass to the main road. My only consolation was that I now had custody of the research vehicle. I could go anywhere I wished just as long as I kept my speed down. This, as I'd learned from Ambrose, required a certain aptitude. The glasshouse on wheels had been especially designed to put individuals to the test. Now, apparently, it was my turn. As I eased onto the road and headed west I realised the great weight of responsibility that had been placed upon me. If I exceeded 20mph the glass would break. Therefore I needed constantly to exercise caution, composure and restraint. Ambrose possessed other qualities too which I resolved to try and emulate: he was decisive, determined, self-disciplined, tolerant and generous to other people (even people who were foolish, feckless, deluded or downright disagreeable). I was just pondering all this when I noticed three men standing at the roadside desperately trying to flag me down. They were wearing beach robes and sunglasses.

Printed in Great Britain
by Amazon